A SMALL ZOMBIE PROBLEM

A SMALL ZOMBIE PROBLEM

⇥ ZOMBIE PROBLEMS · BOOK 1 ⇤

K. G. CAMPBELL

ALFRED A. KNOPF
NEW YORK

THIS IS A BORZOI BOOK PUBLISHED BY ALFRED A. KNOPF

Copyright © 2019 by K. G. Campbell

All rights reserved. Published in the United States by Alfred A. Knopf, an imprint of Random House Children's Books, a division of Penguin Random House LLC, New York.

Knopf, Borzoi Books, and the colophon are registered trademarks of Penguin Random House LLC.

Visit us on the Web! rhcbooks.com

Educators and librarians, for a variety of teaching tools, visit us at RHTeachersLibrarians.com

Library of Congress Cataloging-in-Publication Data
Names: Campbell, K. G. (Keith Gordon), author.
Title: A small zombie problem / K.G. Campbell.
Description: First edition. | New York : Alfred A. Knopf, 2019. |
Summary: When August DuPont, eleven, leaves his eccentric Aunt Hydrangea's crumbling mansion for the first time ever, he meets family, makes a friend, and attracts a zombie.
Identifiers: LCCN 2018026943 (print) | LCCN 2018034695 (ebook) |
ISBN 978-0-553-53957-8 (ebook) | ISBN 978-0-553-53955-4 (hardcover) |
ISBN 978-0-553-53956-1 (glb)
Subjects: | CYAC: Recluses—Fiction. | Eccentrics and eccentricities—Fiction. |
Loneliness—Fiction. | Zombies—Fiction. | Orphans—Fiction. | Supernatural—Fiction.
Classification: LCC PZ7.1.C33 (ebook) | LCC PZ7.1.C33 Sm 2019 (print) |
DDC [Fic]—dc23

The text of this book is set in 12-point Simoncini Garamond.
The illustrations were created using watercolor and colored pencil.

Printed in the United States of America
June 2019
10 9 8 7 6 5 4 3 2 1
First Edition

To Debbie and Rick, who
inspired the whole thing

CONTENTS

PART I

CHAPTER 1   A Bloodcurdling Scream 3

CHAPTER 2   Upon a Fainting Couch 9

CHAPTER 3   The Wild Child 16

CHAPTER 4   Stella Starz (in Her Own Life) 22

CHAPTER 5   The Secret Mission 28

CHAPTER 6   The Far Above 35

CHAPTER 7   The Ghost of Locust Hole 41

CHAPTER 8   The Balloon and the Skeleton 46

CHAPTER 9   The Rabbit-Toothed Visitor 50

CHAPTER 10 An Invitation Is Extended. 56

CHAPTER 11 An Invitation Is Accepted 60

CHAPTER 12 Boy Meets World 67

CHAPTER 13 The Tombs of Hurricane County 74

CHAPTER 14 Château Malveau 79

CHAPTER 15 A Matching Pair of Relations 87

CHAPTER 16 The House of Eternal Mourning 95

CHAPTER 17   The Temptation 102

CHAPTER 18   Boom! 111

PART II

CHAPTER 19   The Risen Dead 119

CHAPTER 20   The DuPont Treasure 125

CHAPTER 21   A Clammy Obstacle. 131

CHAPTER 22   Goodnight's Funeral Parlor. 137

CHAPTER 23   A Small and Icy Hand 145

CHAPTER 24   Madame Marvell 154

CHAPTER 25   The Zombie Stone 160

CHAPTER 26   The Necromancer's Sister 168

CHAPTER 27   The Tattooed Gemologist 175

CHAPTER 28   An Overdue Makeover 183

CHAPTER 29   The Belonging 190

CHAPTER 30   The Betrayal. 198

CHAPTER 31   A Catastrophic Misunderstanding 206

CHAPTER 32   The Evil Twin. 212

CHAPTER 33   Alone . . . Again 219

EPILOGUE 225

PART I

CHAPTER 1

A BLOODCURDLING SCREAM

Thunder rumbled and lightning flickered across the troupe of skeletons: a gruesome, silent circus of grim clowns and tumbling, hollow-eyed acrobats. Skulls gleamed. Skinless faces grinned madly. Bony fingers extended toward the lone, living boy before them.

The boy who had made them.

These weren't *real* skeletons, you understand, but models the boy had built. Their ribs and femurs had been crafted from coat-hanger wire, their skulls from clay molded over Ping-Pong balls. The spindly frames were painstakingly wrapped in strips of paper dripping with a paste of flour and water. When dry and hardened, the papier-mâché had been sanded to a finish smooth as ivory.

The figures stood about sixteen inches tall and wore festive costumes cobbled together from old bandannas, misplaced buttons, and other odds and ends. The ringmaster sported a top hat made from a wine cork and held a chopstick baton. The trapeze artist's swing had once hung in a parakeet's cage. The strongman boasted an impressive mustache of steel wool and boots fashioned from black duct tape.

The boy was engrossed in creating the latest addition to this bizarre, theatrical group. Hunched over a rickety desk, working in the murky light of a stormy afternoon, he was oblivious even to the sound of a sudden shower pattering on the roof above his head.

Beneath his fingers, the model was nearing completion. Its costume was cut from the satin lining of an old waistcoat and studded with tarnished sequins. The hat was a solid silver thimble. The face was painted with particular care. He was outstanding—so splendid, in fact, that the boy had already given the clown a name.

"Nearly there, Kevin," the boy advised. "You just need a nose."

Now, you're probably thinking that Kevin is a rather everyday sort of name for a clown. Clowns, after all, generally come with whimsical names like Tickles or fancy foreign ones like Punchinello. But to be fair, the boy had little experience in thinking up names for things, and Kevin was one of the few he had come across.

He carefully positioned a red plastic pushpin over Kevin's face when suddenly the desk lurched beneath the boy's elbow, jarring the pin from his tweezers and sending it tippy-tapping across the floorboards.

"Aw, shoot!" cried the boy, scrambling after the tiny thing. "It's the last one; where'd it go?" A scarlet speck nestling in a crevice of the rough floorboards caught his eye. "Relax, everyone, I found it!" he reassured his bony audience.

While he was on his knees, the boy added another thin book to the stack supporting one of the desk's broken legs. He pressed firmly on the desk's drop-down front to test its stability.

"All right. Here we go." The boy made a second attempt to center the pin-nose. His breathing slowed. His eyes narrowed. He gripped the tweezers firmly but gently. This was the finishing touch; it had to be perfect!

But Kevin the oddly named clown was not destined to receive his nose that day.

For suddenly, without warning, the wet afternoon was pierced by the sounds of smashing, crashing, and a loud and terrible, bloodcurdling scream.

* * *

"August!" shrieked a woman from the lower floor. "AUGUST!"

Tweezers, pushpin, and stool flew in all directions as August (for such was the boy's name) jumped up. His boots pounded on the stairs as they raced toward the kitchen, from where the screams were coming.

There, a dramatic scene confronted him. You'd be forgiven for concluding that a brutal crime had just occurred, for the room was strewn with overturned crates and broken bottles. The linoleum, range, and icebox were spattered and dripping with bloody red fluid.

But the powerful, vinegary aroma and sting to August's eyes revealed the substance to be nothing more sinister than . . . hot sauce.

Skittering and spinning about in the crimson pools on the floor, the skirts of her ballgown swirling around her, a woman was swatting frantically at a small yellow butterfly. It bobbed above her crooked pink tiara while she continued to screech at the top of her lungs, as if under attack by a pterodactyl.

"August," the woman cried with desperation, "help me!"

But August was saved the trouble of rescuing the lady. He had scarcely passed through the doorway when the butterfly abruptly abandoned its assault and casually flitted across the pungent wreckage to alight purposely on the boy's head.

The woman, finally silenced, observed this unusual development with blanched face and gaping mouth.

"Aunt Hydrangea?" said August with concern.

But there was no response. The lady's eyes rolled upward into her head, and she promptly keeled backward, stiff as a board, in a dead faint.

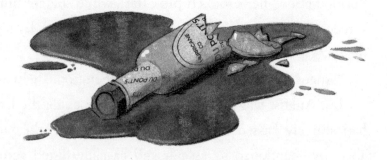

CHAPTER 2

UPON A FAINTING COUCH

When August entered the parlor a few minutes later, the thunder was a distant murmur, and the rain reduced to a steady drip.

"How about," he suggested quietly, "some fortified tea?"

He placed a laden tray on an upturned fruit crate. It served as a table beside a threadbare fainting couch, where his aunt had been settled to recover.

Hydrangea was not young, but nor was she exactly old. A pink tiara perched atop her untidy nest of vaguely colored hair, and a sash diagonally crossed her torso, embroidered with golden thread forming the words "Miss Chili Pepper Princess." The battered headdress was missing many a rhinestone, and the sash was faded and frayed from decades of daily wear.

The lady was perched tensely, her dark watery eyes bulging, her twitching lips forming unspoken words. A flimsy lace handkerchief was getting a good twisting between white-knuckled fists, which rested in the cloud of her voluminous skirts.

"Is it gone?" inquired Hydrangea, fixing August with a terrified stare. "That . . . *thing*?"

"The butterfly exited the way it likely entered," August reassured her. "Through a broken windowpane. I'm sure it was just trying to escape the rain."

"*A broken windowpane?*" Her voice was shrill. "Oh, August, have you secured the breach? You have? I swear, I would not survive another assault. I feel fragile as a glass basket. Please, sugar, check that *this* room is secured; we might be moments from another invasion."

August sighed, nodded, and crossed the parlor, deftly avoiding a large black hole in the floor, where rotted timbers had collapsed into the damp basement below.

It was by no means a modest parlor, high-ceilinged and spacious, with tall windows framed in richly carved rosewood. But the place had clearly seen more prosperous times. There were no dainty chairs with skinny legs. No plush Turkish rugs. The peeling walls were checkered not by fine paintings, but by squares of less faded paper where fine paintings had once hung. The marble mantel was broken and bore no fragile vases or silver candle-

sticks, but only a handful of mildewed family photographs and a porcelain clock whose little goatherd had lost his head.

"The barricades seem secure," August reported, inspecting the boards nailed across the tall windows. "No holes!"

"Then come," said Hydrangea, relieved, her posture relaxing a little. She patted the seat beside her. "Join me." As the fainting couch provided the only seating in the room, August had little choice.

He leaned over the fruit crate to prepare the beverage. Into a chipped cup he poured steaming tea, then added *plop! plop!* two lumps of sugar and, straight from the bottle, a shot of bourbon. He stirred in the finishing touch: a liberal dash of hot sauce. Fortified tea.

Hydrangea sipped. The cup chattered in the saucer, gripped by shaking hands. But the lady's eyelids drooped. She heaved a heavy sigh and grew tranquil.

"DuPont's Peppy Pepper Sauce," she reflected several moments later, "really was the finest hot sauce, August. Have I ever told you of the many awards it won? The accolades? The praise?"

"Many times, ma'am," said August.

Hydrangea nodded toward the hot sauce bottle, and August, familiar with the gesture, obediently coaxed a drop of the brilliant liquid onto his open palm and brought it to his tongue.

"Can you taste the oak barrels?" asked Hydrangea eagerly. "The aged vinegars, the spicy dance of three peppers, and the sweet surprise of hibiscus honey?"

August really could. He nodded.

"Like a dragon's kiss," he said, smiling, quoting the company slogan, knowing that it pleased his aunt.

"Fiery yet sweet," agreed Hydrangea. "Complex yet simple. The perfect hot sauce. No need to rely on sensational names"— she paused, a bitter expression darkening her face—"or novelty bottles, like certain . . . *other* . . . brands."

"You know," she mused, "there was a time when DuPont's Peppy Pepper Sauce could be found in every fine dining room and restaurant from Croissant City to Paris, France. It was without compare."

Her eyes glistened, and August knew from experience that his aunt was revisiting happier days gone by.

"When I was a girl," she said to no one beyond August's shoulder, "the DuPonts were still a family of consequence, on every invitation list. This house, oh, August, you should have witnessed the glittering parties hosted here at Locust Hole. Champagne. Music. Laughter."

The twinkle faded in Hydrangea's eyes as she drifted back to the present.

"Observe us now," she said, gazing around the room. "The

pitiful remains of a distinguished dynasty: a crazy old spinster, a strangely afflicted boy, and a crumbling ruin. We are, I fear, the last of the DuPonts."

She placed her palm upon August's cheek.

"Just you and me. We have no other kinfolk in the world, August. But at least we have each other."

The hand dropped to her lap. Hydrangea lowered her eyes.

"How will we survive, sugar," she said, voice ragged, "after the last of DuPont's Peppy Pepper Sauce has been sold? Why, only a few dozen crates remain. And as you know"—she shot the boy a sad, resigned smile—"there is no more in production." A frown creased her forehead. "Curse that fluttering devil! So much wasted sauce; every lost drop is a penny down the drain. Oh, August, I'm so sorry. It lunged at me from nowhere, and naturally I panicked and upset the crates."

"Naturally," repeated August, although he felt pretty certain that a crippling horror of butterflies was anything but natural. But he assured her, nonetheless, that she was being fretful and should not worry about their circumstances and that everything would be fine.

But he wasn't sure that it would.

"Remind me again," he suggested, attempting to check his aunt's rising agitation, "how you won the county Chili Pepper Princess pageant."

At this proposal, Hydrangea visibly brightened. She set down her tea and, smoothing her sash, opened her mouth with an eager expression. But before she could speak, the broken porcelain clock announced the hour with a strangled, rusty chime.

"What?" cried August sharply. "It's four o'clock *already*?" He leaped to his feet, rattling the tea tray and startling his wide-eyed aunt. "I'll help you clean up later," he blurted. "I have . . . um . . . an appointment!"

"With whom," declared Hydrangea, astounded, "could *you* possibly have an appointment?"

But the boy was gone.

CHAPTER 3

THE WILD CHILD

The door of August's room slammed behind him as he charged toward his splintered desk. Hastily he yanked open and rummaged through the drawers. Not there. He scanned the Formica-topped table, where the skeleton circus stood assembled. Not there either. He pushed aside the stuff from which the grinning performers were built: coat hangers, vintage newspapers, a large jar of Ping-Pong balls. Nope, nothing.

"Shoot!" cried August in frustration. "Now, where did I leave it?"

He cast about frantically, extending his search across the entire garret. A garret (in case you didn't know, and why would you because you probably don't live in one?) is a cramped sort of room huddled beneath a building's roof. It's the sort of dismal lodging preferred by bedraggled painters and poets who wallow in the gloom, supping thin porridge and creating "important" art.

And while this may sound a bit depressing, the garret suited August just fine. He had, in fact, only recently claimed the space as his own, abandoning a much grander room with a fireplace on the first floor. It was true that the raw beams made for constant ducking and skull thumping. And indeed, much of the space was occupied by balding leather trunks, towers of musty storage boxes, and discarded household objects, including an old ironing board and a keyless piano. But the room had one unique and beneficial feature: it could be accessed only by a narrow staircase that Hydrangea's expansive skirts could not pass.

And so, above the realm of his aunt's rules and barricades, August was able to glimpse the world outside from two small, unboarded windows that pierced the roof at front and back.

From this lofty outlook, the vista seemed vast and fascinating. But in truth the house inhabited a quiet, forgotten corner of the county. Indeed, the dirt road ended at Locust Hole, giving few people reason to venture there. Occasionally an intrepid tourist, the kind who travels alone in comfortable shoes, might set up his fancy camera on a tripod to take atmospheric pictures. Beyond that, the grocer's delivery boy, the mailman, and the critters of field and swamp provided the only comings and goings there were to observe.

Until recently.

"There you are!" exclaimed August with relief. A pile of empty Mudd Pie wrappers (August had a particular fondness for the cookie snacks) lay discarded near the wastebasket. Beneath these, August retrieved the object of his search: a telescope. He snatched it up, dashed to the rear window, opened it, and placed the smaller end of the instrument to his eye.

Through the age-speckled lens he first scanned the field behind the house: a sorry, spartan stretch of dirt sprouting withered, wilting pepper plants. At its far end he located the crooked frame of the ruined gazebo, where long-ago DuPonts had dined alfresco on long-ago balmy evenings.

Beyond *that* lay the narrow canal. And there in the muddy water, rocking gently, was the most recent addition to August's small world. It had arrived without notice a few weeks prior, moored by someone in the dead of night. It was a houseboat.

Although, *houseboat* might be a generous description. It was, in fact, little more than a large shed roped to a wooden pallet, buoyed up by a pontoon formed from old oil drums. A rusting contraption with pipes and dials sat on "deck." This, August concluded, must be the generator by which the floating home was lit and powered.

The houseboat seemed perilously pitched, one end weighted down beneath a tired-looking outboard motor. August did not believe the ramshackle vessel looked seaworthy.

He was, however, greatly intrigued by a crudely painted sign nailed to its wall. Garish colors had faded to shadows, but August could just make out the words "Madame Marvell, Ball Gazing, Magic + More."

He wasn't exactly sure who Madame Marvell was. In the days since the houseboat's mysterious arrival, August had observed only one crew member with his telescope: a scrawny barefoot girl with a tangle of unbrushed hair. She spent her days grubbing about the canal bank collecting frogs in a colander, filling the generator from a spouted can, and dozing facedown, limbs loose like an unstrung puppet in the branches of nearby trees.

The girl seemed so entirely at ease in the untamed landscape, so like a creature of nature, that August had begun to think of her as an untamed thing. Wild. He suspected that this wild child was not the Madame Marvell mentioned on the sign. But without another person around to claim the name, he had attached it to the girl, and somehow it seemed to fit.

At that moment, August spotted her scrambling onto her floating home, one arm cradling her colander, the other a bunch of freshly plucked iris.

"We're both running late, Madame," August muttered. "Hurry now; it started five minutes ago!" He swiveled his telescope just a tad, following the girl as she passed inside. "No! NO!" he cried in anguish as the flowers were dumped into a pitcher at the houseboat's window, blocking his view.

But a sigh of relief followed as the flower arrangement was moved, revealing beyond it a small, boxy, old-fashioned television. And, as the screen flooded with static, then color and life, the hairs on August's arm tingled, and his heart jolted with the thrill of excitement.

You see, while the houseboat and its inhabitant had enlivened August's sleepy landscape, this scuffed-up TV, with its plastic knobs and crooked rabbit-ear antenna, had changed August's *life*!

CHAPTER 4

STELLA STARZ (IN HER OWN LIFE)

Every Monday and Thursday at four o'clock, Madame Marvell's dusty television screen opened a window into another world, a world that, previously, August had no idea existed.

It was a colorful, exciting, intoxicating world. It was the world of *Stella Starz (in Her Own Life),* a twice-weekly TV show surrounding the madcap misadventures of a California teen. Madame Marvell—and now August—were regular viewers.

Now, it's not that August had *never* watched TV. In fact, in the kitchen there was a half-decent plasma screen Hydrangea had ordered from a catalog and would often turn on after dinner. But August's aunt was very particular about their viewing choices, being easily agitated by shows containing heated confrontations, loud noises, and outdoor settings, where one might encounter butterflies and other "dreadful things."

Hydrangea preferred programming with more predictable events, static, indoor environments, and, preferably, "educational content."

"I have a responsibility, sugar," she would explain defensively, "to your homeschooling."

Game shows, with their routine format, familiar sets, and informative content, checked all the boxes. And indeed, his exposure to *Are You a Dummy?, Win It or Lick It,* and *Word or Number?* had left August well versed on world capitals, breeds of fancy chickens, notorious outlaws, and many other fascinating facts about the world beyond Locust Hole.

His aunt would certainly never have permitted August to watch a show like *Stella Starz.* She would have been highly alarmed by the way the heroine careened through the world with carefree enthusiasm (Hydrangea would have called it *reckless abandon*), recovering stolen penguins, forming rock bands, unmasking school librarians as spies, and generally placing herself in overwrought situations where she had no business being.

Madame Marvell's window was generally left ajar, so the voices of the actors and the dramatic soundtrack often drifted faintly across the parched field to reach August's ears. But even when the vessel was shut up, or when the breeze carried the television's sound away from Locust Hole, it wasn't that difficult for the boy to decipher what was going on.

And he loved the zany, sometimes gripping exploits of Stella and her friends. He got that Stella's surname was a play on words that could subtly alter the meaning of the show's title. *Stella Starz (in Her Own Life)* was a show about a girl with the surname Starz and the life she leads. *Stella* Stars *in Her Own Life* was a show about a girl who shows up, to live her life to the fullest.

Had August shown up to live his own life? He didn't think so.

Stella's crazy, roller-coaster existence could not have been more different from his own, and it enthralled him. So captivated was he that August always remained glued to the show through the closing credits, which rolled over the same series of stills: snapshots of Stella and her friends engaging in familiar, spirited high jinks. The very last frame lingered longer than the rest. It had etched itself into August's memory, and the image would often float into his mind before sleep.

This time was no different. Stella and her friends were gathered at a lunch table. Behind them milled an out-of-focus throng of students with trays. In the foreground, two boys were thumb-wrestling. One girl peered into her phone, giggling. Another tossed kettle corn into her own mouth. Stella herself was facing her best friend, Kevin (yes, that's right, *Kevin!*), her hand raised to meet his, in an exuberant high five.

There was something in the scene that made August feel

warm inside. The group at that table seemed so happy. So complete.

They belonged.

August wanted—*really* wanted—someone to high-five.

August wanted to belong.

When Madame Marvell's screen returned to a dull, opaque green, August's room seemed even quieter than it had before. Emptier.

"Hey," August said over his shoulder, to his own Kevin. "You want to share a Mudd Pie?" But the noseless, lifeless clown didn't answer. No one answered. August was alone. As ever.

And why, you ask, was this boy always alone? Well, as you may have begun to suspect, August DuPont had never passed through his own front door.

At almost twelve years old, August DuPont had never left his house.

CHAPTER 5

THE SECRET MISSION

August would normally have hung out a little longer to see what Madame Marvell did next. After the show, the wild child often sat on her deck, enjoying a supper of fried frogs' legs (don't make that face; it remains a very popular dish in some parts), or holding animated conversations with a large cloth doll that appeared to serve as her only companion.

But Monday was an eventful day (at least by Locust Hole standards), and there were other things to observe. A butterfly had perched on his telescope, so August swatted it outside, closed the window, and promptly crossed the garret. The front-facing window was set into a fanciful little tower, roomy enough for a small bench with cushions, which permitted August to settle more comfortably and peer out.

The front yard was much smaller than the back. Only forty feet or so from the front porch, a weathered picket fence was collapsing beneath an overgrown, shrubby hedgerow, and beyond it lay the dirt road. Pressing his forehead against the windowpane and squinting to the right, August could see the steep slope of the embankment built to contain the fickle, unpredictable waters of Lost Souls' Swamp. Beyond the grassy ridge, from the tops of the cypress trees, a snowy-chested osprey rose from its smudge of a nest and squealed shrilly as it soared over Locust Hole.

Quickly reversing his position, and squinting to the left, August watched the bird flap across the glinting waters of Black River, then the distant steeple and power lines of Pepperville. The osprey shrank, increasingly difficult to distinguish against the brownish clouds towering over the horizon, where August knew the Withering Wetlands gave way to the Pirates' Sea.

The approaching sound of wheels on wet dirt abruptly returned August's attentions to the lane. He dropped the spyglass and glanced down to see a tousled head of ginger curls gliding unsteadily above the shrubs.

"Grosbeak's!" announced August with satisfaction.

The grocer's delivery represented Locust Hole's second big event of the day. You will appreciate that to a boy who never went anywhere, even the most routine occurrences held enormous interest. Prior to Madame Marvell's arrival, the Monday delivery from Grosbeak's General Store & Soda Shop had been the highlight of August's week. The boys (and one girl) who regularly deposited paper bags on the front porch represented August's only real-life glimpse of people his own age.

In recent months, the battered black bicycle with the Grosbeak's sign had been ridden by a sturdy, freckle-faced youth with a blunt nose and sleepy eyes. August watched him dismount by the gate and struggle to release the kickstand. The large, heavy basket above the front wheel was unwieldy, and an awkward skirmish between boy and bike ensued.

Lugging a brown bag in each arm, the boy headed through what was left of the Italian garden: a flat, gray shadow of the geometric pattern once formed by paths, hedges, and flower beds. He glanced apprehensively up at the house—more specifically, toward the roof.

The garret window was small, grimy, and cobwebbed. It seemed unlikely to August that an outside spectator could have seen through it. Nonetheless, he shrank back into the gloom.

Having deposited his delivery, the redheaded boy descended the porch steps, and August observed a rip in the seat of his pants. It was likely, August concluded, the result of some violent tumble, for the boy was an appalling cyclist. Not that August (never having ridden a bicycle himself) was an expert. But Stella and her gang were forever tearing about on flashy beach cruisers and mountain bikes, so he had some idea of how it should go.

He watched the boy depart, weaving and wobbling down the lane, like a drunken june bug. August grimaced, silently wishing the boy a casualty-free journey.

And with that, the day's activities were over.

August sighed and was turning away when he noticed something amiss. On the ground near the gate lay a small box, printed in navy and yellow. It must have fallen from the overloaded grocery bags. August knew exactly what was in that box. Indeed, it was all too familiar, for such boxes contained his weekly supply of Mudd Pies.

In fact, while watching *Stella Starz* minutes before, he had absently devoured the last of the addictive, chocolate-covered, marshmallow-filled cookies from the prior week's delivery.

There were no more.

Except those resting in a puddle outside.

Outside, where his aunt Hydrangea would not venture.

No more Mudd Pies for a week.

August stood deathly still, staring at the box for a full minute. And in that very short time, the box evolved into something more than a box, something more important. It became . . . a mission!

"Someone," he said quietly, to no one, to everyone, "needs to rescue that box."

* * *

The front-door barricade was devised to be easily removed, at least partly. Two of the lower planks could be lifted from their brackets, permitting one of the double doors to be opened. Squeezing through the resulting space, Hydrangea could retrieve the groceries or infrequent letters that were left on the porch, with minimal exposure to butterflies and such.

Now, August slipped his fingers beneath the lower plank and lifted, causing a significant scraping noise. He paused, listening. The muted tinkle of broken glass and sounds of sweeping from the kitchen assured him that his aunt was still busy cleaning up the hot sauce wreckage.

August lifted the second, waist-height plank.

The key moved, with some resistance. Over the course of a hundred years, how many DuPont hands had turned it? As his sweaty palm gripped the cold, smooth doorknob, August gasped for air and realized that he'd been unconsciously holding his breath. He wondered if his heartbeat might have sounded as loud to a bystander as it did to himself.

The knob twisted.

The latch released.

The door cracked open with a plaintive, unsettling creak.

He paused again. Aunt Hydrangea was singing now, some melancholy ditty from bygone days, her thin, shrill voice wavering in volume. *"After the ball is over, after the break of morn, after the dancers' leaving, after the stars are gone . . ."*

August opened the door.

He was engulfed by a waft of warm, damp, earthy air. Through the opening, not ten yards away, he could see the navy-and-yellow box of Mudd Pies. It would take only moments to retrieve it.

Did his aunt need to know? It might even be better if she did. Sure, she'd be horrified at first. But a successful mission might help to convince her that her many fears were unfounded.

Right?

August crouched in the doorway, his heart pounding. It seemed so vast out there. So endless. With no ceilings to contain him, would he just float off into space? Were there truly as many dangers as his aunt insisted?

He decided he didn't care. He needed to know for himself.

And just like that, for the first time in his life, August Du-Pont stepped outside.

CHAPTER 6

THE FAR ABOVE

The sky above remained heavy with storm clouds, but stand-ing at the foot of the porch steps, August was still blinded by the unfamiliar outdoor glare. He covered his face with his hands and slowly separated his fingers, letting his eyes gradually adjust to the outdoor light.

Finally, by shielding them with his open hand, August's sight began to return. He was immediately confronted by some twitching, fairy-like thing near his nose, and it took the boy a moment to identify the creature as . . . you guessed it, a butter-fly! The insect bobbed around his head with a lazy, contented air. It was shortly joined by another. And another.

Wincing in the light, August lifted his head to watch them. Far above, beyond the gathering butterflies, brilliant against the gray heavens, a colored dot caught his eye. It was a balloon, bright orange like a nearly ripe chili pepper, adrift on a tropical current.

For her birthday party, Stella Starz's father had filled the house with so many colorful balloons, the guests could scarcely see each other. Things began to go noisily awry when festive sparklers met with the fragile air-filled orbs, causing many of the balloons to explode. The drama escalated even further when her father's girlfriend, Hedwig, accused Stella of stealing her cell phone.

Stella (and August) were deeply offended by the charge, and it seemed that the celebratory event might have ended abruptly in bitterness and disaster, until a muffled ringtone revealed Hedwig's phone to have been inexplicably baked into the birthday cake.

"Stupid Hedwig," Stella and August had both muttered.

August wondered if the orange balloon above him had floated away from such a party. He imagined himself grabbing its string and being carried off, back to the place it had come from, a place with sparklers and friends who high-fived and shared each other's Mudd Pies.

Mudd Pies! August's mind returned to the task at hand. He located the navy-and-yellow box, boldly leaped across several puddles, and was bending to retrieve it when something un-expected caught his eye.

In the squelchy rain-drenched dirt, a distinct and deep impression had been left. It was a footprint. A footprint of something nonhuman. A footprint with five clawlike toes.

"Scary Reptiles" had once formed a category on *Win It or Lick It*. From what he had learned on that episode, August recognized the print as that of an alligator. But what alligator had a foot the size of a car tire? How enormous would such a creature be?

A sudden sound frightened August half to death. But he instantly realized it was not that of some monstrous animal; it was, rather, distinctly human. It was the sound of someone gasping. Urgent whispering followed.

August straightened to be confronted by a face peering at him through the tangle of swamp rose and sumac that arched above the yard gate. Beyond it lay two more faces, one smothered with freckles and framed by a mass of ginger curls.

All three wore openmouthed expressions of utter astonishment, as if observing a polka-dotted zebra.

But in fact, *this* is what they saw.

* * *

August DuPont was a wiry young fellow but a little small for his age. He was not particularly remarkable in any feature, other than his eyes. They were unusually large and round and rendered even larger and rounder by large, round eyeglasses. Even more memorable was their singular color: the palest gold, like late-summer marsh grass.

His nose and mouth were, by comparison, quite small. Someone observing him might be reminded of a baby owl.

But perhaps most astounding of all, and the thing that had provoked such astonishment in his small audience, was the cloud of twenty-odd butterflies that were fluttering in contented circles around August's owlish head.

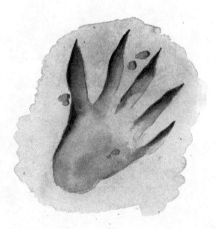

CHAPTER 7

THE GHOST OF LOCUST HOLE

August was, in short, petrified.

He had never spoken to a person other than his aunt Hydrangea, never mind been thrust face to face with three strangers. He remained frozen for a millisecond, then turned to flee.

"Wait!" called a young voice, not unkindly. "We won't hurt you. Promise!"

August's instinct would have propelled him on, but something powerful and important stopped him in his tracks. Hands clammy with fear, he slowly turned to face his spectators.

"I *told* you it would work!" exclaimed the ginger-haired delivery boy. "I told you there was a ghost at Locust Hole. I *told* you he'd come out to fetch that box. No one who eats that many Mudd Pies is going to just leave them sitting in a puddle!"

"Well, you finally flushed him out," admitted the lanky youth who brought up the rear. Heavy-lidded eyes and an unsmiling mouth lent his long face a sleepy yet solemn expression. "It took long enough; this is our third attempt. I was beginning to think you were plain crazy."

"I *said* I'd seen him up at that roof window," said the redhead, grinning triumphantly, "lurking in the attic, like ghosts do. Everyone in town says there's a ghost boy at Locust Hole. And I got him!"

"Gaston! Langley!" said the third stranger forcefully. This boy had far-apart eyes of brown, very dark, but translucent like breakfast tea. In striking contrast, he had light hair, the color of honey. A curious fitted garment that buttoned to one side covered his entire torso. It looked like it might be padded and designed for some sort of sporting activity.

"How many ghosts," he asked, "do you know that eat Mudd Pies?" The delivery boy folded his arms and pouted a bit. The tall boy bobbed his head from side to side, acknowledging the reasonableness of the question.

"Are you a ghost," said the blond boy directly to August, "or not?" He gave a devilish yet good-natured smile.

Throughout their exchange, the three strangers had not

taken their eyes off August, and still they stared, waiting eagerly to hear him speak.

"I'm just a human being," said August in a small, hoarse voice he hardly recognized, "like you."

"Then how," asked the tall one accusingly, pushing back his dapper brimmed hat with one finger and waving another generally in August's direction, "do you explain the bugs?"

August shifted uncomfortably, scratched his upper arm, and swatted a butterfly away from his face.

"Um . . . so I have this rare condition. I guess," he said.

"Speak up!" said the delivery boy, wiping his nose on his sleeve. "Can't hear you."

Remember that August had spent his whole life until now in the dusty quiet of his aunt's company. He had never been required to raise his voice in order to be heard.

"Rare condition," repeated August, his voice catching as he consciously turned up the volume. "My skin emits this scent that attracts butterflies. I mean, *you and I* can't smell it. No one can. Except butterflies. It's supposed to be kind of like flower nectar. The butterflies really like it. They don't bother me, though; it seems to make them sort of sleepy."

This announcement met with a stunned silence. The boys at the gate had clearly little experience with such *unexpected* conversations. Still no one spoke, and August sensed that things had gotten a little awkward, so he plunged in again.

"My case," he explained, "is particularly unfortunate. My aunt Hydrangea, she's who takes care of me, she suffers mightily from a phobia of butterflies. Can't abide them. She won't even venture outside because she fears them so. She doesn't let me go outside either because, well . . ." He waved his hand vaguely at the throng of insects around him and shrugged.

The honey-haired boy, the one with some air of authority, was the first to gather his senses after August's extraordinary revelation.

"What's your name?" he said to August gently.

August smiled shyly and opened his mouth to speak, but he didn't have to.

"August!" shrilled a hysterical voice from inside the house. "AUGUST! There is an intruder within. Oh, save me, August! SAVE ME!"

CHAPTER 8

THE BALLOON AND THE SKELETON

August rifled through his old desk's many cubbies and drawers, all stuffed with the kind of household junk that accumulates, gathering dust for decades: yellowing bills and invoices, tarnished sports medals, rusted hatpins, and solitary playing cards.

"I'm certain I saw . . . ," he mumbled. "Aha! Here it is." August withdrew a plastic net bag containing a collection of random marbles and, opening it, withdrew the largest.

It was a beauty, the size of an apricot. The vivid amber glass with a swirl of jet-black at its center reminded August of an alligator's eye. Marbles this enormous, he knew, were sometimes referred to as "toe breakers," for the damage they might cause if carelessly dropped on one's foot.

Before him, August placed a rigid, vertical wire, with a large coil at bottom to serve as a stand. Using mounting glue, he adhered the huge marble to a smaller loop at the top of the wire.

The wire stand was twisted and painted brown to resemble a string. In reality, it supported the heavy glass marble, but it *appeared* to dangle from it, the end trailing on the ground.

To support the illusion of weightlessness and flight, August had added a boy-sized skeleton with unusually large, round eyes. A tiny paper butterfly perched upon its head. The skeleton boy's fist tightly gripped the "string," and his feet were inches above the tabletop. The model was clearly designed to suggest the boy was being carried off by an orange balloon, to some unknown place and adventure—a party perhaps.

August sat back to admire his creation and the light refracting through the amber marble. It was his best model to date, surpassing even the clown Kevin in detail and beauty. Lately, you see, he had had plenty of spare time to work on it.

One solitary butterfly, the "intruder within," had revealed to Hydrangea that the front door had been opened, and worse, that her nephew was . . . *outside!* She had discovered him bounding up the porch steps, trailed by a flurry of airborne monsters.

The woman had promptly declared herself "unraveled as a porcupine's sweater!" and withdrawn (with the front-door key) to her bedroom, where she had spent two days weeping and torturing lace handkerchiefs. All homeschooling had been

suspended, and other than frequently preparing trays of fortified tea, August had been left to his own devices.

Given the fragility of Hydrangea's condition, August had decided it best to keep the encounter with the boys at the gate to
himself. It would be easier on his aunt's nerves, he thought, to
process one out-of-the-ordinary occurrence at a time.

But Hydrangea's recuperation was about to be roughly ter-
minated.

A sudden, jarring, metallic jingle resounded throughout the
hollow spaces of Locust Hole, causing August to jump violently.
He rushed to the staircase landing, from where he could see the
hallway below. Hydrangea stumbled from her room, disheveled,
wild-eyed, and ashen.

"What *is* that sound?" hissed August.

"Why . . . I," stammered Hydrangea, flustered and confused,
"I believe it's the doorbell!"

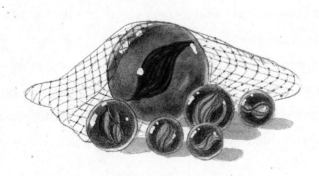

CHAPTER 9

THE RABBIT-TOOTHED VISITOR

The planks were removed. The key was turned. The door was opened, just a crack. Hydrangea stooped to regard Locust Hole's first visitor in August's memory.

"Mr. LaPoste?" Hydrangea's voice contained more surprise than alarm, which, in turn, thoroughly surprised August. The door opened fully.

"Miz Hydrangea?" said a man's voice, and August saw a face peering in through the waist-high opening.

With entirely unexpected force, Hydrangea grabbed the man's bag strap, yanking it and him through the opening, and slammed the door behind him. The thin fellow in a blue uniform stumbled forward, then straightened, and August recognized him as the mailman he had occasionally studied from his garret lookout.

If a wicked fairy were ever to turn a rabbit into a person, the result would certainly resemble Mr. LaPoste. He had pale, staring eyes, an itchy-looking pink nose, and an overbite of very large, very white teeth.

His expression revealed that he was startled by his sudden arrival in the foyer . . . but not shocked. In fact, on regarding Hydrangea, he broke into an immense, enthusiastic, toothy grin.

"Why, don't you fret, Miz Hydrangea," he assured the lady fervently, "I do not travel—nor have I *ever* traveled—in the company of butterflies!" He turned in a circle, still smiling broadly, to prove it. "I arrive here entirely insect-free!"

Hydrangea blinked rapidly, momentarily speechless. But August detected some small change in her demeanor; she appeared to recover her senses and, straightening her tiara, sank into a theatrical curtsy.

"Mr. LaPoste, what a delight!" she declared in elegant tones. "Your call is unexpected, but most welcome."

The mailman returned the greeting with a deep bow and flowery hand gesture.

"Miz Hydrangea," he said, shaking his head in wonder. "You haven't changed one little bit since the old days. Why, you're still as fresh and pretty as a swamp rose in July."

"Oh, come now, sir," said Hydrangea in a silly, giggly voice that August had never heard and found jarring coming from his aunt. "You play fast and loose with the truth." She flapped her handkerchief at nothing in particular, and swished her skirts from side to side. "But I did have my moments, I suppose. Do you recall the glorious summer I won the county Chili Pepper Princess pageant?"

LaPoste nodded. "Uh-huh," he said, a little vaguely.

August wondered if he really did remember. Perhaps he was just being kind. The victory, after all, was probably less memorable to anyone other than Hydrangea.

"I do beg your pardon," blurted LaPoste, abruptly changing the subject, "for this unheralded intrusion. I would have left the mail on the front porch as usual"—he rummaged in his bag—"but could not permit such a genteel person to imperil herself in attempting to retrieve it."

Hydrangea was quite unused to having her anxieties so bluntly validated. With eyes bulging, she clutched at her heart.

"*Imperil*, Mr. LaPoste?" she cried with anguish. "Whatever can you mean?"

"There have been sightings, Miz Hydrangea," said LaPoste in hushed tones, "in these parts, of an alligator."

"Well, that is not so peculiar." Hydrangea had unconsciously lowered her own voice. "Alligators often find their way into Black River from Lost Souls' Swamp, is it not so?"

"But this, Miz Hydrangea, is a mighty uncommon beast. Witnesses claim that the thing is pure white. Yes, a *white* alligator! Who'd have thunk of such a thing? And its size, they say, is monstrous, upward possibly of forty feet."

"Forty feet!" exclaimed August, remembering the gargantuan footprint he'd discovered in the front yard.

LaPoste jumped, clearly unaware that there had been a third party listening nearby. When he caught sight of August peering from the lower staircase, his eyes widened and his pink nose twitched.

"So, it's true," he said in quiet wonder. "There *is* a boy!"

Hydrangea turned and ushered August forward.

"Come, sugar," she said to her nephew, but smiling at their guest. "Where are your manners?" August stepped cautiously into the light.

"You must excuse him, sir," simpered Hydrangea. "We receive so few callers at Locust Hole these days; our manners are a little rusty." She waved her handkerchief at the man, then the boy. "Mr. LaPoste, meet my nephew August, last of the DuPonts."

The mailman reprised his operatic bow.

"It's a pleasure, sir."

August nodded with a half smile.

"Well then," said LaPoste, withdrawing an envelope from the bag, "*this* delivery suddenly makes a bushel more sense."

Aunt Hydrangea reached for the letter. The mailman's grin stiffened awkwardly.

"Um . . . the letter is not for you, Miz Hydrangea." He turned and held the envelope toward the staircase. "It's addressed to Mr. August DuPont."

CHAPTER 10

AN INVITATION IS EXTENDED

As Hydrangea gushed her farewells and thanks to the departing mailman, August perched on the parlor fainting couch, oblivious to an old spring poking his rear end. He turned the envelope in his hands. The stationery was thick and creamy, like parchment. It seemed expensive.

"I can hardly comprehend it," exclaimed Aunt Hydrangea, entering the room. "No one has ever laid eyes upon you. How could they possibly be aware of your existence? How could they know your name? You've never spoken to another soul in the world."

"Well," said August, wincing, "actually . . ."

With flushing cheeks, he reluctantly shared the history of his meeting at the gate.

Swaying, Hydrangea grabbed at the back of the fainting couch and lowered herself to the seat.

"To be sure, we are undone," she whispered, handkerchief pressed to her cheek. "For so many years, I have endeavored to keep the world out of Locust Hole." She glanced at August reproachfully. "And in one foolish instant, you have let it in."

They both automatically looked at the envelope.

The innocuous thing practically buzzed with significance. Whatever lay inside, they both understood, was an invasion from the outside world. It was a knife that was about to slice open their carefully woven cocoon.

Heart thumping, August slid his finger beneath the flap and withdrew the contents, a thick sheet of notepaper. He unfolded it to reveal a family crest, embossed in metallic gold, the sight of which elicited an audible gasp from his aunt. The crest depicted a shield, emblazoned with the image of a chili pepper impaled on a fancy-handled dagger. Fluttering banners proclaimed the words "Malveau. In Riches Unrivaled."

Below all this, a note had been handwritten, in what August guessed was ink from a fountain pen. The penmanship was simultaneously elegant, confident, and intriguing. August was immediately anxious to meet its maker. He read the note aloud.

Dear Mr. DuPont,
    You are cordially invited to join me for

afternoon tea, here at Château Malveau,
tomorrow at four o'clock.
    It would be my pleasure to know you.
             With warm regards,
             Orchid Malveau

"I declare!" breathed Hydrangea in a hoarse gasp. "Oh my!"

August studied his aunt, baffled. "Do you know who this Orchid Malveau person *is*?"

Hydrangea grimaced and, working her handkerchief, shot August a nervous glance. She nodded. Was that *embarrassment* in her expression?

"I do. Orchid Malveau . . . is my sister."

CHAPTER 11

AN INVITATION IS ACCEPTED

August wrinkled his nose, puzzled. "But you don't *have* a sister," he said plainly. "We have no other kinfolk in the world. Just you and me. Remember?"

Hydrangea stood and, skirts rustling, moved toward the mantel.

"We *don't* have any other family," repeated August less certainly, "do we?"

Hydrangea's head turned. Her eyes met her nephew's. August could see something unfamiliar in her red-rimmed eyes. Could it be guilt?

"*You* said," growled August in a dangerous, unfamiliar voice, "we were the last of the DuPonts."

"And so we are," responded Hydrangea, with slight defiance.

"My sister Orchid forfeited any claim to the DuPont name when she married a Malveau."

"*You* said we have no other kinfolk in the world."

"Well, I," shrilled Hydrangea, defensively, "am the only kin that *loves* you!"

"How"—August's voice grew loud with outrage—"could this sister—my *aunt*—love me, if she's never even *met* me?"

Hydrangea plucked at her handkerchief as if removing the petals from a daisy. "The Malveaus love nothing," she muttered sulkily, "except money and prestige." She paused. "They imagine their great wealth elevates them, to some superior status."

"Great wealth?" repeated August, intrigued.

"Great wealth," snapped Hydrangea, looking up sharply, "built on treachery and betrayal! The Malveau family is the source of all our misfortunes."

She paused. August raised his eyebrows, with an "okay, go on" expression. Hydrangea considered the boy for a moment, clearly weighing her next words. She launched in.

"It all began more than a hundred years ago, before Locust Hole was even built. Two men—cousins, best friends—left their faraway home to seek their fortunes in this country."

As she spoke, Hydrangea clutched her handkerchief with both hands and strode about the room, absently avoiding the hole in the floor.

"One cousin, Maxim Malveau, was idle and arrogant. The other, Pierre DuPont, was industrious and smart.

"Pierre had arrived with a pepper plant from his mother's garden, which he planted, cared for, and propagated. Hot sauce had yet to reach these shores, so using his mother's recipe, Pierre created the nation's very first! And oh my, August, it was a huge success: DuPont's Peppy Pepper Sauce became a household name, and Pierre found himself a rich man.

"Pierre was a generous fellow and happy to share his success with Maxim. Despite his cousin's lazy indifference, Pierre instated him as factory manager with a handsome salary. Maxim should have been forever grateful for his cousin's loyalty. But no!"

Hydrangea spun to face August, her finger pointing accusingly.

"Instead, he *stole* it!" she hissed. "Maxim Malveau stole the recipe for DuPont's Peppy Pepper Sauce. He opened his *own* factory, selling his *own* hot sauce, claiming it was his *own* concoction and renaming it Malveau's Devil Sauce."

Hydrangea stopped pacing. "His one original idea," she reflected bitterly, "was to devise a gimmick: that hideous bottle with demonic horns. And people liked it. They like it still. It certainly sells." She opened her palms, as if baffled.

"But, Aunt," said August, shrugging, a little confused, "all of that happened so long ago. How can you still—"

"The Malveaus," said Hydrangea, now quiet and deadly serious, "have been our bitter rivals ever since. They have been

bent on the destruction of DuPont's Peppy Pepper Sauce, and indeed of the DuPonts in general. And it seems"—she glanced around their ragged surroundings—"they are nearing success."

The lady returned to the mantel and studied the headless goatherd.

"When my sister," she continued, "chose to marry a Malveau—to embrace our mortal enemies—it broke our papa's heart. He barred Orchid from Locust Hole and disowned her. We all did. I've seen nothing of her for over thirty years."

"That seems," said August, frowning, ". . . rather harsh."

Hydrangea ran her finger around the goatherd's jagged neck.

"You haven't met your aunt Orchid," she said with a small, sour smile.

"Were you never friends?" asked August.

Hydrangea considered this.

"When we were children, I suppose," she admitted begrudgingly. "Long before your dear mama, our baby sister was born. We spent many a stifling, summer's day escaping the heat, hunting for family treasures in the forgotten corners of Locust Hole."

Hydrangea's face clouded.

"But as the family's fortunes dwindled, Orchid changed. She yearned for the parties and pretty things of the old days. She became selfish and greedy, always striving to be the best, have the most.

"You know"—Hydrangea turned to August with an expression of indignation—"Orchid actually entered the Chili Pepper Princess pageant . . . *to compete against me!* My own sister betrayed me, just as Maxim betrayed Pierre. Orchid was well qualified to become a Malveau."

August wasn't entirely sure that the two offenses were of equal gravity. But his aunt clearly thought they were, so he kept the sentiment to himself.

The parlor fell silent, other than the clock's soft ticking. Dust twinkled in the meager light that penetrated the barricades. Hydrangea, her fury spent, shot a sideways look at her nephew. He was glumly staring at the invitation in his hands.

Their eyes met.

"I want to join the world, Aunt," said August. "I want to see things, and do stuff, and meet people."

"But, child," protested Hydrangea, sweeping to the couch beside the boy. "The world is such a hazardous place. So many dangers. Remember the mighty alligator of which Mr. LaPoste spoke."

August thought of the tire-sized footprint in the mud.

"It might at this very minute," Hydrangea hissed, "be lurking beyond our own gate, with dripping teeth and an empty belly." They both glanced toward the front door in the foyer. "And even if it isn't, what of the hordes of dreadful butterflies; there's your . . . your *condition* to consider!"

August said nothing for a moment, thinking.

"I'll take the necessary precautions," he assured his aunt.

Hydrangea abruptly sat back, her eyes wide with surprise at this quiet but forceful resistance. Something important was happening between them, some fundamental shift in power.

"I'm lonely, Aunt Hydrangea," said August simply.

Hydrangea stared at the invitation, now clutched to August's chest like a life preserver. When she looked up, her eyes were glistening.

"My dear boy. I swore to your mama on her sickbed that I'd protect you. I haven't kept you cooped up here in Locust Hole for any reason other than—"

"I know, ma'am. But it's time for me to . . . to show up to my own life. I'm sorry if Maxim betrayed Pierre. I'm sorry if Aunt Orchid betrayed you. But it was all a very long time ago. Maybe she's different now." He gave her an apologetic smile. "I *am* going to Château Malveau."

Hydrangea's shoulders slumped, and they both understood that things had changed forever. August would no longer be contained. The aunt nodded sadly, patting her nephew's arm.

"Do as you must," she said. "But heed my warning, August. Orchids are exotic and very lovely. But some of them are deadly poisonous."

CHAPTER 12

BOY MEETS WORLD

At three o'clock on Thursday, August passed through the gate into the lane. He paused to unfold the tattered driving map that Hydrangea had handed him at the front door. The wrapped box under his arm—a gift for Aunt Orchid—made the process rather awkward, and he was further hampered by the bulky beekeeper's gloves and netted helmet his aunt had insisted that he wear.

"To safeguard you from those tiny monsters," Hydrangea had said, delivering an enthusiastic grin that did little to conceal her terror.

And indeed, the "protective" clothing seemed to mask August's unique scent sufficiently that his entourage of butterflies was reduced to two or three.

The boy waved the insects away so he might locate Château Malveau on the map. Having established the route, he lifted his head and, for the first time, got a good look at Locust Hole from the outside.

At some point, largely from watching television, August had come to understand that his home was unusually shabby and worn. But it was only upon regarding the building's exterior from a distance that August came to appreciate its true level of decay.

It had been a finely built, handsome old house, with a broad, shady porch. Typical of that low-lying region, it was built on raised foundations, to spare the main floor from flooding and provide a half basement for storing the pepper barrels.

But the roof was balding, and it sagged where one of the slender posts supporting it had splintered. Shutters that weren't nailed closed hung at crazy angles from one hinge. Most of the pretty blue paint had peeled away, and the clapboards beneath had been bleached to pale gray. Unchecked vines snaked through the railings, and the squat basement doors beneath the porch were rotting and green with moss.

Another decade, and Locust Hole would likely qualify as an actual ruin.

Aunt Hydrangea stood outside the front door. August knew she would venture no farther. From the gate she looked much smaller. Vulnerable. She raised her arm and weakly waved her handkerchief.

August returned her salute with a confident thumbs-up, turned, and walked away.

* * *

It didn't take very long for the heat to catch up with him.

The boy had been too absorbed with his map and giddy with adrenaline to notice it immediately. But as he crossed the rusty local bridge that spanned Black River, August found his breathing labored and rivulets of sweat trickling across his ribs. You see, in summer months, towering banks of air from the Pirates' Sea would roll across that place, smothering it with a blanket of thick, salty humidity.

Locust Hole, punctured as it was by patched-up holes, still largely sheltered those within from the sultry climate without. Now beyond its thick old walls, August felt like he was wading through a vapor of hot broth.

He pressed onward, to the main road (such as it was, for as mentioned, this was an out-of-the-way sort of place, and passing vehicles were few). The Old French Highway led into Pepperville, hugging the river's winding passage. But any view of the water was obscured by the fields of blazing pepper plants that flanked the narrow ribbon of asphalt.

Field followed field. Nailed to the fences, sign followed sign, each informing passersby that all they observed belonged to Malveau Industries. How many signs had August passed? How much land did the Malveaus own? How long had he been walking?

He began to feel dizzy. It was too much. Too much at once. The heat. The bombardment of unfamiliar smells, sounds, and sensations. The boy felt overcome and limply slumped onto a large rock at the side of the road, knees weak, head spinning.

He lifted the net of his helmet and covered his ears. He closed his eyes and spent a minute inside himself, recovering in the darkly glowing nothingness.

When he was ready, August took a deep breath. He focused on the faint, flowery fragrance of water hyacinths and the earthy, dank smell of the roadside ditch they sprang from.

Slowly he unplugged his ears, gradually admitting the chorus of the cicadas. Time slowed, and within the insects' buzzing, he heard something rhythmic and melodic, almost like a chant.

He heard the feather-soft flapping of a low-flying ibis headed toward the swamp. He heard the rustling clusters of flame-colored chilis, a million crimson fingers clutching at the tropical breeze.

The warmth of the yellow dirt penetrated the soles of his shoes. The ground seemed to press itself against his feet. Or was gravity pressing him into the ground? Could he feel a dull, distant throb, perhaps the very heartbeat of the earth?

Suddenly someone whispered in August's ear.

His eyes snapped open, and he leaped up in alarm, spinning around to confront . . . whomever he was about to confront.

But there was no one there.

He was alone.

He was, however, facing a sizable clearing, some leafy interruption to the lengthy string of Malveau pepper fields; he could glimpse the twinkling river at the far end. A strange stillness hung about the place, where a cluster of large white stone boxes hunkered in the weeds and unkempt shrubbery. August had been sitting not on a rock but on the broken remnants of a tomb.

He was standing at the edge of a small cemetery.

CHAPTER 13

THE TOMBS OF HURRICANE COUNTY

Hurricane County, and all those counties surrounding it, existed in a particularly soggy part of the nation.

This was a region where the land and sea met, not abruptly as they might at a beach or a seaside cliff, but gradually, insidiously, over many wet, low-lying miles, one morphing imperceptibly into the other. This was a place of elusive islands that might vanish for hours within the mist, or for months beneath the tide. This was a place of deltas and swamps, hurricanes and storm surges. This was a place where water reigned, and nothing could truly be called solid ground.

Any hole you might have cause to dig would certainly flood.

And so it was, that those who died there were laid to rest *above* the ground, in boxy crypts of creamy stone.

* * *

The words had been unclear, but August was certain he had heard a voice.

"Hello?" he called out cautiously. "Is someone there?"

He heard it again. Whispering. It had an insubstantial quality, almost like he was hearing the echo of a sound, rather than the sound itself. But it was close by. Very close. For a second, August wondered if it might even be inside his own head. Was his mind addled by the heat?

He stepped into the tall grass.

"Hello?" August called again. "Where are you?"

The graveyard was forgotten and untended. The tombs sat all higgledy-piggledy, slumping dramatically this way and that into the soft, sodden ground. Many of them bore his own surname, DuPont. Many others contained the remains of deceased Malveaus.

Whisper, whisper.

It was a small voice, perhaps a child's. It was so close. Right beside him, but muffled, as if a wall lay between them.

It was coming from inside a crypt.

This structure was not low and coffin-shaped like the others, but upright and roofed, like a mini Roman temple. There were square columns at the four corners, and perched on top, a precious stone cherub wept into its hands. A large slab was screwed into what would otherwise have been a doorway, engraved with an epitaph that read "Forever our angel, Claudette."

August mounted the single step and pressed his ear to the cold marble. Could a child be somehow trapped in this place?

"Is someone in there?" he called. Nothing.

"Can I help you?" August raised his voice, although it was apprehensive, hoarse.

He sensed a presence. Someone was close by, August was certain, and in need of assistance. He heard a movement, a scraping. Maybe a grunt. Something heavy smashed to the floor.

"Are you all right?" yelled August with great concern. "Are you stuck?"

Were those footsteps? They sounded sluggish and dragging. Uneven.

Suddenly some powerful thing struck the slab from inside with such force that August was knocked to the ground, his helmet tumbling into the grass.

Another massive blow caused a large jagged crack to appear in the stone.

And then the pounding became continuous, violently smashing the marble again and again and again. More cracks

scattered across the stone's surface and it began to crumble around the bouncing screws, small chunks of stone landing at August's feet.

Whatever was in there was about to get out.

And August felt confident that it wasn't a child!

CHAPTER 14

CHÂTEAU MALVEAU

He had run more than a mile. Panting and dripping, August clutched his side and turned around. An empty road was all that lay behind him. He had not been followed.

He regretted panicking so blindly. In the face of encountering . . . whatever that was, his wits had left him. Had he kept his head about him, he might well have fled back to Locust Hole to breathlessly reassure Hydrangea that she'd been right all along: the outside world was far too dangerous a place to explore. But he had bolted without destination or strategy, gift and helmet clutched to his chest, until he found himself at the high metal gates that bore the Malveau family crest: the chili pepper impaled on a fancy-handled dagger.

For obvious reasons, August hadn't had much experience

with distance running. He slumped against a smart iron fence, taking a few moments to gulp air, while studying a large, brown metal sign that confirmed his arrival at Château Malveau, a state historical landmark.

Guided tours of the mansion and Malveau Industries' hot sauce factory were offered on Fridays at 11:00 a.m. August rather wished he'd been invited the following day so he might have taken such a tour.

His heart rate slowing, August straightened and checked his watch: 3:35 p.m. At this time last week, August realized, he had been posted at his rear bedroom window, eagerly anticipating the opening titles of the *Stella Starz* show. He could never have imagined that seven days later, he would be out of doors, embroiled in his own melodrama, recovering from an alarming graveyard encounter and minutes from meeting some mysterious aunt.

Despite the weakness in his knees and the pounding in his chest, August smiled.

But the second hand was ticking and the butterflies were gathering, so with a final swipe at his hot, wet brow, the boy replaced his helmet, tidied up his package, and passed through the open gates.

* * *

It took August almost as long to travel the dirt driveway as it had to reach the entrance in the first place. The entire route was flanked by towering oak trees, whose arching branches met above him to form a cool and leafy cathedral. The colossal girth of their trunks suggested they had stood here for centuries, long before any house had been built.

Great sheets of Spanish moss drifted from the gnarled tree limbs, curtain after curtain obscuring the view ahead. But eventually, wispy gray tendrils parted to reveal the driveway's destination: Château Malveau.

On catching sight of the mansion, a thrilling shiver raised the hairs on August's arms and neck. He had never seen anything so magnificent. Stella Starz had once located a small, misplaced prince, and even the castle where his royal parents had hosted a thank-you banquet seemed modest by comparison.

Slender Greek columns supported generous wraparound verandas. Graceful French doors opened onto airy balconies. The steep roofs were crisply shingled, and soaring turrets reached for the sky as if it were actually within their grasp. All seemed freshly painted in creamy white. Imagine a fairy-tale palace spun from the sparkling icing of a wedding cake, and you'll get the idea.

But for all its ambitious beauty, there was a sadness to the place. The drapes beyond those graceful French doors were closed up, obscuring any peekaboo view of the interior. Everything was utterly and completely still, as if time did not exist here. No sound. No breeze. A peacock, unusually jet-black,

strutted stiffly across the path. Upon spotting August, it opened up its splendid tail, lifted its head, and emitted its piercing cry, strange and filled with sorrow.

* * *

The front door was opened by a toad-like man in a snowy-white jacket. If a neck supported his flat, widemouthed face, it was concealed by his starched collar and black bow tie. Although he was barely taller than August, he somehow contrived to regard him down the length of his squat nose. He eyed the circling butterflies with a raised bushy eyebrow.

"Um, good afternoon?" said August uncertainly.

"Excuse me, sir?" replied the man, leaning in with a hairy, pink ear. "I can scarcely hear you."

"I am here," bellowed August so loudly that the man jumped. Then, more meekly, he added, "To have tea with my aunt, Orchid Malveau. Who are you? I'm August DuPont. Are we also related?"

"*Related?*" The man recoiled, staring at August's outstretched hand in horror. "I am Escargot, sir. *The butler!* May I take your gloves and . . . um . . . *hat?*"

* * *

The mansion was equally splendid on the inside. A cavernous central hallway stretched from front to back. Above twinkled glass chandeliers, the kind that had once been powered by gas. Below gleamed mahogany floors, partly covered by old, fancy rugs.

Near the baseboard, decorative grilles delivered cool air, which was all the more delicious for the oppressive summer heat outside.

The walls were hung with portraits of Malveaus from long ago . . . and not so long ago. They stared out from their gilded frames, dark-eyed, unsmiling, all sumptuously costumed in fine clothing and jewels.

Escargot came to a stop before a wide pair of sliding doors and, with a gloved hand on each knob, pushed them into the walls on either side. Though very large, they were well oiled and opened with ease.

"Mr. August DuPont!" the butler declared importantly to the room beyond.

August entered a grand salon as the doors closed behind him.

The ceiling was painted with a delicate fresco of curlicues and shells. Above the mantel towered a great mirror, oddly draped in sheer black fabric that obscured the room's reflection. Every corner and surface was crowded with bronze statuettes, candlesticks dripping with crystals, and vases filled with clouds of sweetly scented flowers. The walls, settees, and tufted chairs were all covered in the same soft green damask fabric.

It was a lofty room, and it might have been bright too, had

the draperies not been closed. Some amount of sunlight did trespass between the heavy, patterned panels, piercing the interior with a glistening, speck-filled shaft. In this half gloom, the olive-colored interior resembled an underwater grotto. August almost expected a catfish to wiggle past his face.

There was so much to look at, so many "sunken" treasures, it was several seconds before August noticed there were other living people present. Clearly neither, however, was Hydrangea's sister. Rather, seated on a green settee was a girl around his own age. Beside her, his arm draped leisurely across the mantel, stood a boy.

August recognized him immediately.

It was the honey-haired boy he'd encountered at the gate of Locust Hole.

CHAPTER 15

A MATCHING PAIR OF RELATIONS

August's eyes traveled from the boy to the girl and back to the boy, and he blinked in surprise to see the same face in duplicate; the two were clearly twins. Two pairs of wide-set eyes, dark but translucent, like breakfast tea. Two heads of that singular, tightly waved blond hair. Two full mouths with curving lips that looked like they'd been drawn by an artist. The symmetry and proportions of their oval faces were so perfect, they reminded August of paintings he'd seen in a documentary about the Italian Renaissance.

They were dressed, August realized, entirely in black—the girl oddly formally, in an expensive-looking dress and high socks; the boy in the same unusual athletic garb as before. In his fist was the grip of a thin silver sword, which he held upright, casually resting on his shoulder, its point sheathed within a protective rubber tip.

"Do you fence?" the boy inquired, lowering the weapon and crossing the room with an outstretched hand, which August—with little choice—shook. "It's a gentleman's sport, you know; all stamina, strength, discipline."

He flexed the slender blade, which sprang back and forth with a pleasing twang.

"A foil, they say, requires the most skill; points are earned by hitting specific targets on your opponent." He jabbed August's ribs gently with the soft rubber tip. "But I'm a saber man myself. You just slash away, left and right, really go to town!"

The foil quickly and loudly sliced the air around him as August blinked nervously, wishing that he too were safely buttoned into a trim, padded jacket.

"Um," he said apprehensively. "Who *are* you?"

The boy froze mid-thrust, mouth open.

"Why . . . you don't *know* yet?" He looked half-shocked, half-amused. "It seems we are related, August. Just discovered the fact ourselves, no more than an hour ago." He drew himself up, with a broad, enthusiastic grin. "I," he announced with impressive confidence, "am Beauregard Malveau." He extended

his open palm toward the green settee. "This is my sister, Belladonna. Orchid Malveau is our mother."

"My aunt . . . is your *mother*?"

"That's it. We are your cousins."

August was stunned. Cousins. What?

"I didn't realize," he stammered, shyly thrilled, "that I *had* cousins." He glanced at Belladonna.

The girl was seated behind a small table cluttered with the stuff of crafting: bottles of glue, paintbrushes in jelly jars, newspaper to protect the tabletop. The pungent, acrid odor of some potent substance stung August's nostrils.

"What did he say?" Belladonna inquired of her brother.

August repeated himself more audibly (and made a conscious note to speak with more volume in the future).

"We knew nothing of you either," responded Belladonna absently, slowly rising and moving toward August, her eyes fixed on something above his head. She drew close, peering intently upward, mouth ajar. August got a good eyeful of her unusual necklace, a string of shiny, black-lacquered, chunky tubes that looked strangely familiar.

"Is that . . . a *butterfly*?" said Belladonna in wonder.

"Is that . . . rigatoni?" asked August.

Belladonna's gaze fell sharply to August's face, and her mouth snapped shut. She retreated coolly, fingering her necklace.

"My sister," said Beauregard, raising his eyebrows knowingly, "fancies herself a jewelry designer. She works exclusively"—he stifled a half smile—"in pasta!"

"I make things too," said August hopefully. But Belladonna had returned to her worktable, with a sideways glance appraising the butterfly's owner. August was suddenly very conscious that his jacket was a size too small, and he realized how dusty his boots must be after the long trek.

"Do you believe me now, Belladonna," appealed Beauregard, "about the butterflies?"

But the girl merely sneered and returned to her creative endeavor.

"She's notoriously hostile," explained Beauregard. "You know"—he leaned over, nudged August's thigh with the foil's guard, and whispered into the boy's ear—"when there are twins, one of them is always evil, right?"

He winked, and August experienced a surge of delight. Stella Starz and her gang were constantly exchanging winks, confirming one another's status as co-conspirators, insiders; confirming that they *belonged*.

No one had ever winked at August before. It felt warm and welcoming, like he was being admitted to a secret society. Still, he shot a nervous glance at the evil twin. But she was stubbornly engrossed in lacquering a large piece of cannelloni.

"I promise you," said Beauregard, placing a firm grip on August's shoulder and nodding toward his sister, "that not all the Malveaus are so frosty. You are very welcome here, Cousin. You are part of the family now."

August smiled bashfully.

"In fact"—Beauregard straightened, eyebrows high, clearly struck by a brilliant idea—"you *must* be our guest at the annual crawfish boil. We host it at Château Malveau every year."

Belladonna's head jerked up. She glared at Beauregard. She glared at August.

"Beau!" she barked with an expression of shocked contempt. "You can't be serious." She held out her palm toward August. "He's obviously—"

"Ignore her," interrupted Beauregard as August flushed with embarrassment; it was clear that Belladonna didn't think much of him.

"It's real fun," Beauregard reassured August kindly. "There's a band. And dancing. A whole mess of things to eat. And this year, Mama's letting us play paintball! It'll be the perfect opportunity to introduce you to the crew!"

"You sail?" asked August.

Beauregard and his smile paused. *"Crew!"* he repeated with emphasis. "Like posse. Entourage. Gang. *Friends!*"

Friends? Gang? August's heart skipped a beat. There was a gang!

Beauregard was studying August with a puzzled and slightly concerned expression.

"So . . . how peculiar are you, exactly? I mean, the butterflies are curious enough as it is, but they give you some personality, I guess. I think I can sell them. But there's nothing even stranger, is there, that I should know before I take you on? Nothing unpleasant or gross? No sleeping in coffins? No monsters in the cellar?"

"Uh . . . no . . . I . . . ," stammered August, feeling vaguely like he was being interviewed for a job he hadn't applied for.

"The Malveaus," said Beauregard more seriously, his smile less broad, "have a certain reputation in these parts. Ours is the finest, most powerful family in the county. We wouldn't want anything—or anyone—to be associated with us that wasn't . . . respectable. Normal, you understand?"

August thought about his highly strung, tiara-wearing aunt. He thought about his boarded-up house and his squalid attic bedroom and the fact that at nearly twelve years old, this was his first venture beyond the garden gate. He thought about the alarming incident in the graveyard.

"Nope," he said quickly, shaking his head with confidence. "Everything else is perfectly normal."

Beauregard's face lit up again, and he gave August's shoulder a friendly shake.

"A whole new cousin," he said, beaming. "A DuPont, no less."

August's hand twitched. Surely this must be the right

moment. He swung his open palm into the air. But August's first high five would have to wait. At that very moment, the doors again slithered open to reveal the neckless butler.

"Miz Orchid," bellowed Escargot, "awaits Mister August in the Chamber of Jewels!"

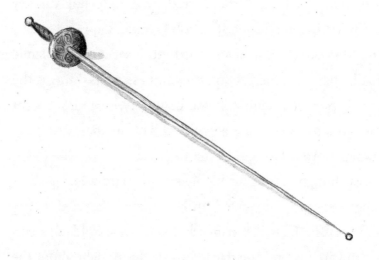

CHAPTER 16

THE HOUSE OF
ETERNAL MOURNING

The Chamber of Jewels had clearly been designed as a library, with walls of rich mahogany shelving that scrambled from floor to ceiling. And indeed, a small collection of ancient, leather-bound books still inhabited some lower areas.

But most of the available shelf space had been given over to the display of gemstones. Each was protected by a glass dome and sat upon a round wooden plinth with a small metal plaque to identify the contents. Museum lights recessed into the underside of the shelves illuminated the specimens beneath and cast the room in a ghostly glow.

As he appeared so far to be alone, August browsed the

collection. Some of the gems were as you might expect: gloriously hued, and cut with many glittering facets. Others were smoothly surfaced and opaque. Still others looked like any rough, commonplace rock you might kick down the street or throw down a well.

A few of their names were familiar: amethyst, fire opal, yellow sapphire. Others had more exotic, intriguing titles: meteorite, bloodstone, zebra rock.

One specimen in particular caught August's attention. It bore the name tag "Cadaverite." But it was not the stone that arrested him; rather, it was the stone's *absence.* Despite the labeling, the display was empty.

August found something inexplicably tragic about this vacant dome and the undeniable fact that something was very much missing.

He was contemplating possible explanations when, from the corner of his eye, he noticed a slight movement. August turned to observe a palmetto fan wafting gently back and forth. It was held by long, slim fingers—fingers that belonged to a person seated in, and concealed by, one of the high-backed chairs angled toward the fireplace.

August was not, and had never been, alone.

Softly rustling, the figure rose from that shadowy part of the room. It was a woman, extravagantly dressed in a lengthy, black silk gown. An elaborate, high black comb protruded from the back of her predictably honey-blond hair. Her entire personage, from comb to ankles, was draped in a veil that glittered with tiny black seed pearls.

Behind the black lace lay twinkling black eyes, a fine nose, and enigmatic, rose-colored lips. August would not have been surprised if the woman had introduced herself as queen of the underworld.

But she didn't.

Instead, she tilted her head and examined the boy with curiosity.

"There was gossip, of course," she said in a voice as warm and creamy as café au lait, "surrounding the ghost of Locust Hole. But then, ghost stories are not uncommon around these parts and rarely credible."

August could see some resemblance to Hydrangea. The women shared a similar height and frame and must logically have been close in age. But where Hydrangea seemed limp, fragile, and exhausted, the air around this woman buzzed with some vital, magnetic energy.

"It was only," she continued, "after Beauregard returned with his report—you met your cousins, yes?—that I deduced this so-called phantom could only be Lily's child. It was rumored that my youngest sister had given birth, but all assumed

that the baby was taken—along with its mother—by the epidemic."

With a soft expression, the woman reached out and absently touched August's cheek.

"You're like her," she said. "At least, from what I recall. She was just a girl the last time I saw her. Before I . . . left."

"I don't remember her," said August, speaking more loudly in order to be heard the first time.

"It was so long ago," agreed the woman. "And yet also like yesterday. The Peruvian flu was a democratic disease, I will give it that, claiming the lives of rich and poor alike. Men. Women. Children too."

She looked away, toward the shuttered window, the fan rippling her veil.

"It took my husband, you know," she said. "It crushed my heart. It emptied the world of happiness, of music, of color."

She glanced briefly around and gestured at their surroundings.

"And so we wear black. And close the shutters. We cover the mirrors." Her chest rose as she sighed deeply. "Ours, child, is a house of eternal mourning."

"You must have loved him very much," said August.

The woman's gaze was fixed on something in the past, in sadness. Her black eyes burned with something fierce and awful.

"I was robbed," she said in a voice raw with grief and fury

that sent a shiver down the boy's spine. "I would do anything to recover what I lost."

For a moment, the room was horribly silent. And then, as if suddenly returning to the present, the woman started slightly and, facing August, smiled. She extended her fingers in a regal manner that suggested they should be kissed. Navigating the huge black diamond rings, August did so.

"I," quietly announced the woman, "am your aunt Orchid."

"I brought you a gift," blurted August, presenting his now rather crumpled parcel.

Orchid Malveau laid her fan and August's box on a table topped with black marble and delicately unwrapped the gift. From the tissue, she withdrew a model. It depicted a skeleton boy being carried aloft by a large orange balloon.

August was suddenly painfully aware of the opulence surrounding them. His model instantly seemed out of place and foolish. Ridiculous, even.

"I made it myself," he muttered.

"How . . . enchanting." Orchid's smile seemed forced. She moved to the mantel and pushed aside a lush potted fern, replacing it with the skeleton boy. "I shall treasure it forever."

Orchid's genteel politeness somehow made August feel even worse. He nodded, deeply embarrassed.

Orchid seemed sympathetic to his plight.

"I'll have Escargot bring us tea," she said gently, twisting a brass S-shaped handle affixed to the wall. On its release, August heard the muffled sound of a bell somewhere deep within the bowels of the mansion.

"In the meantime, child, come sit here. I have a proposal for you!"

CHAPTER 17

THE TEMPTATION

The marble-topped table was repositioned before the fire-place, and on it, tea was served. The DuPonts' finances were such that scrimping and saving was the norm, and dining at Locust Hole was necessarily a humble affair. August, therefore, had never sat before such a sumptuous spread as this. You see, afternoon tea at Château Malveau was not just tea.

It did indeed include a pitcher of sweet tea, but also a pot of fragrant chicory coffee. And towering above the beverages were tiered silver stands, crammed with mouthwatering delicacies: wafer-thin pralines, crustless crawfish sandwiches, and airy beignets dusted with powdered sugar.

August was wondering if he'd overloaded his plate, and

whether or not he should tuck his napkin into his shirt, when Orchid reopened the conversation.

"So, child," she said, coffee cup in one hand, saucer in the other (she had lifted her veil sufficiently to permit food and drink), "what do you make of my collection?"

"Of gemstones?" said August absently, deciding which tantalizing morsel to try first. "It's very comprehensive."

Orchid returned her cup and saucer to the table.

"This . . . hobby, I suppose you might call it," she said with a tragic air, "is the only thing that brings me anything resembling pleasure. It fills my waking hours. Indeed, I have spent *years* acquiring a specimen of every gemstone in the world." She heaved a heavy sigh. "Except one."

There was a moment's silence. August had a thought.

"Cadaverite?" he suggested.

"Why, aren't you observant," said Orchid with a small smile. "Clever boy. Cadaverite is the rarest of all minerals. Nearly impossible to locate and recover. Only a handful of fragments exist." She paused, tapping the arm of her chair with one finger. "But it just so happens that I know where one may lie!"

August's mouth, at that moment, was too full to respond. In the subsequent silence, he became suddenly aware of the deafening crunching coming from inside his mouth (the pralines were irresistible). He smiled sheepishly, cheeks bulging, forced a gulp, and licked the stickiness off his teeth.

"Oh?" he mumbled with polite interest.

Wordlessly, Orchid leaned forward and opened a drawer in the tea table. From it, she retrieved a pamphlet that was about the width and height of a magazine but merely a few pages thick. She handed it to August.

He wiped his fingers on his napkin, then found himself inspecting a theater program. It was very old, the paper thin and brittle, the faint, brownish color of withered petals. Large text in a curly font read "Croissant City's own Théâtre-Français presents . . ."

Below this was a black-and-white photograph of a man with a twirled mustache emerging through a circular frame. He wore a bow tie with old-fashioned evening clothes and an exotic-looking tasseled hat. He held one hand aloft, fingers spread in a dramatic gesture. The other hand gripped a polished black staff, topped by a large, rough stone or fossil, whose natural shape vaguely resembled that of a human skull.

But most intriguing of all was the man's face.

Although depicted without color, his eyes were clearly pale and piercing, unusually large and round and rendered even larger and rounder by large, round eyeglasses. His nose and mouth were, by comparison, quite small.

He reminded August of nothing more than a baby owl.

Croissant City's own
Théâtre-Français
presents
Orfeo DuPont
Master of morbid magic!
August 8-9, 15-16, 1919 7p.m.
25c

With a mustache.

Beneath the portrait, the text continued, ". . . Orfeo Du-Pont, Master of Morbid Magic."

"You can see, no doubt," said Orchid, "that he is your ancestor. You're rather like him, you know."

"Am I?" August considered this. "He seems a little . . ."

"Theatrical?"

August nodded.

"The DuPonts," said Orchid with a humorless expression, "have a history of"—she paused, searching the ceiling for the right word—"*colorful* behavior. Our ancestry includes more than its fair share of oddballs and spendthrifts who have, over the years, squandered the family fortune, reducing Locust Hole to its present sorry state."

"Aunt Hydrangea," said August cautiously, "says that . . ."

"That some long-dead Malveau stole the DuPont hot sauce recipe?" suggested Orchid with a wry smile. She rolled her eyes.

"It is a century of poor judgment, child," said Orchid bluntly, "that has led to the demise of DuPont's Peppy Pepper Sauce. Not some legendary theft from yesteryear. Generation after generation, the DuPonts have repeatedly pursued their foolish fancies—such as becoming a pageant princess—rather than attending to the family business."

Orchid twisted her mouth.

"How is that swimmy-headed sister of mine, anyway? Still celebrating her bygone victory and sporting that ridiculous pink tiara?"

August shifted uncomfortably in his seat, caught between loyalty to Hydrangea and a sudden desire to discuss her eccentricities with this woman who knew her so well. He said nothing, but in doing so, said everything.

"I thought as much," chuckled Orchid. "And even *you,* I understand"—she glanced at the butterfly settled peacefully on August's forearm—"have a certain . . . *uniqueness.*"

She leaned forward and tapped the theater program on August's lap.

"Orfeo is the perfect example of DuPont self-indulgence. He was far more concerned with magic and theater than hot sauce."

August flushed slightly, feeling chastised. Watching him, Orchid's expression softened. She relaxed, letting the tension clear.

"But I didn't invite you here, child," she spoke gently, "for a history lecture." Her gaze intensified. "*Here,* August, is the interesting thing."

She took the playbill and, facing it toward the boy, pointed at the magician's staff.

"This stone? The skull-shaped fossil?" She paused for effect. "It's Cadaverite!"

August peered more closely.

"And DuPont family legend would have us believe"—
Orchid's voice was now close to a whisper—"that the thing is se-
creted somewhere inside Locust Hole. Indeed, when Hydrangea
and I were girls, long before our baby sister—your mama—was
born, we'd spend many a summer's day hunting for old Orfeo's
rock in the forgotten corners of the house."

August looked up.

"All right," he said, unsure what was expected of him.

"We never found it."

August waited, but the woman merely stared.

"And . . . you think it's still there?" August suggested.

"Why not? It's exactly the sort of thing that might wind up in
a family attic, buried beneath decades of discarded possessions—
perhaps at the bottom of a trunk . . . or in the drawer of some
old bureau."

An image of the rickety desk in the garret popped into August's head.

Orchid finally lowered her eyes and, wafting back into her
chair, rested the playbill on the tabletop.

"It might take just a little digging around," she suggested,
breezily waving her hand, "by, say, an inquisitive, observant
young man, to unearth it."

"Ah!" said August, a lightbulb turning on. "You'd like *me*
to look for it?"

"Only if," said Orchid, once again the very image of tragedy, "you have the inclination to bring some scrap of happiness to a grieving widow . . . your aunt."

What could August—or indeed any half-decent person—say to *that*?

"I'll help however I can, ma'am," August said with a polite smile, then frowned, struck by a sudden thought. "But even if the stone *is* still there . . . wouldn't it rightfully belong to Aunt Hydrangea? Didn't she inherit everything?"

Orchid's smile remained utterly unchanged for a few moments, as if she had suddenly transformed into a wax replica of herself. Again, August fidgeted uncomfortably, sensing he had touched a sensitive nerve.

"And what could Hydrangea possibly want," laughed Orchid suddenly, "with such a thing? It's nothing but a dusty old fossil, an ugly rock, of value to no one but a silly, sentimental collector like myself.

"Still"—Orchid fixed the boy's gaze—"we wouldn't want to give my . . . *fragile* . . . sister anything more to fret about, now would we?"

August hesitated, recalling Hydrangea's cautionary words about the toxicity of certain orchids. And Orchid watched him, dark eyes twinkling like a raven's.

"You have doubts," observed Orchid. "Perhaps"—her voice

was low, humming with intensity—"I can offer you some additional . . . *motivation*. A return favor. I could, for example"—her rose-colored smile was intoxicating—"ensure that you are sent to school with Beauregard and Belladonna!"

⟨ ►⟩ CHAPTER 18 ⟨◄ ⟩

BOOM!

"*School!*" August practically shrieked, leaping up and dropping his crawfish sandwich.

Orchid started back in surprise.

"Well," she said defensively, seeming to misinterpret this dramatic reaction, "if you'd rather fester away in a crumbling ruin with that timid mouse of an aunt . . ."

"No!" August assured her passionately. He composed himself and sat down. "No, ma'am; I would not."

His heart was thundering, his eyes bulging with delight. Could this be true? Might he yet, like Stella Starz, star in his own life?

Orchid patted his hand.

"Very well," she said, mildly amused. "You shall attend the

middle school in New Madrid with the twins this coming fall. You are how old? Ten? Eleven? Well, they'll be a grade ahead, but they can still keep an eye on you."

"I'm not sure"—August suddenly looked crestfallen—"if my aunt Hydrangea . . ."

"You let me deal with her, August. There are laws about . . . your sort of *situation*. I'm sure she wouldn't want the authorities involved."

August's brow furrowed with concern.

"It will be fine, child. *She* will be fine. It's simply not proper for a young man like yourself to be shut away from the world, to spend his days lurking in the attic like a ghoul. Don't you agree?"

August did.

"Then we have a deal? School in return for the Cadaverite?"

August contemplated Orchid's outstretched hand. What could possibly go wrong? He reached out and grasped it. Her handshake was like Beauregard's: powerful and self-assured. The Malveau handshake.

There was a rap at the door, and Beauregard's perfect oval face appeared.

"Any pralines left?" he inquired optimistically.

"Come in, child, come in," urged Orchid, rising and gliding toward him. "Help yourself. August and I have completed our business." She paused in the doorway before exiting and half turned her head.

"I am confident, August," she said, holding his gaze from the corners of her eyes, "that you won't let me down." She delivered that hypnotic smile, and August experienced a shiver of apprehension.

"When you're ready, Beauregard will show you out."

*　*　*

August was running again, but this time the heat and humidity were nothing to him, and the exertion felt exhilarating and right. The pepper fields streaked by on either side, but August was oblivious to everything except his unbridled happiness. He was flying!

In one afternoon, he had acquired an aunt and two cousins, a party invitation, and the opportunity to attend school. *School!* The world of Stella Starz suddenly seemed not only less fantastical, but possibly *attainable*!

August wasn't sure, but he suspected that in Beauregard he might even have found his first—dare he think it?—*friend?* Someone to high-five. Well, eventua—

—*boom!*

All at once, August's chin and ribs smashed into the road, and the air was forced from his lungs. It took a moment for the stunned boy to understand that he had tripped, and hard at that.

He lay facedown, wondering briefly if he was still alive. But his breathing returned with a shaky gasp, and there was pain, so he concluded that he must have survived. Inches from his nose, through his helmet netting, he could see a large fragment of peach marble. Carved lettering stretched from one side to the other: "—orever our angel, Clau—"

Groaning, August turned his head to the right. There was the cemetery, and the sweet little temple, a jagged black hole now marring its front. The rooftop cherub was gone, but its head—the face still cupped in its chubby hands—lay in the grass a foot or so away.

Closer still stood two little feet in dainty shoes of white leather.

One sock had collapsed around the ankle. The other stretched to a grubby knee. Above that was a silk dress, very old-fashioned, like the clothes one might see worn in an antique photograph. The garment was faded, frayed, and generally much the worse for wear.

And above *that* was the face of a young girl.

But there was something deeply amiss about her. Her complexion was mottled and gray. Her ringlets were matted with dirt and rubble. Her head hung limply to one side, and her posture

was crooked and awkward, like a leggy foal attempting to stand for the first time. A single strand of spittle drooled from the child's slack, blue lips.

It didn't take a genius to realize, immediately, that this particular little girl . . . was dead!

PART II

CHAPTER 19

THE RISEN DEAD

O r rather, the girl was *undead,* for there she stood, blinking and twitching entirely of her own accord.

August had no time to even consider a reaction before the child bent over, grabbed the back of his jacket, and yanked him to his feet, as if he weighed no more than a kitten.

She was strong. Insanely strong.

The insanely strong, undead, blinky, twitchy girl threw her arms around August, pinning his biceps to his torso. The musty smell of cold stone, mold, and mildew enveloped him. The boy screamed, certain he was about to be crushed to death. But while she held him tightly, the child did August no harm.

Instead, she gazed up at him; well, sort of. Her clouded eyes sought August's face but had a tendency to swivel loosely away, in random directions, independent of one another. Her bubbling mouth formed a lopsided grin, more akin to a leer. But it seemed well intended. If August were forced to interpret the girl's expression, he would have guessed it was one of . . . *adoration*?

August liberated himself from this clammy embrace with considerable difficulty. This child was possessed of the strength, after all, to punch her way out of a solid stone tomb. He raised his palms and took a couple of steps backward, slowly, for fear of startling her.

The blue lips moved slightly, and August heard a thin, gur-gling whisper—the same whisper he'd heard from inside the mausoleum.

Then suddenly, without invitation, the girl reached up to her face and, with a revolting squelch, removed her left eyeball and offered it to August, as if it were an everyday gumball. The slimy gift was accompanied by an encouraging grin.

August, staring with horrified awe at the cavity in her skull, shook his head.

"Um . . . thank you," he said, mouth very dry. "But I'm good." He waved a finger at his own face. "I already have my own." He backed up a little more. "I should be heading home. It's late."

He turned in the direction of Locust Hole and took a few

steps, glancing nervously behind him. The child followed, eyeball outheld.

"I said no thank you," called August. "You should stay here."

Still she followed.

August stopped and turned.

"Go away!" he said firmly. The eye remained obstinately offered forth.

Not wishing to lead her home, or back to Château Malveau, August headed into the cemetery. He sped up. She sped up. He swerved right. She swerved right. He lunged left. She lunged left.

August made a dash for it. He sprinted as fast as he could, zigzagging between the tombs, the sound of thrashing grass and weeds all around him. He went deep into the graveyard, almost to the river, then doubled back toward the road, finally smashing through a hedge of buttonbush and hurling himself behind a large tree.

He collapsed onto his behind, panting, then listening. No sounds of pursuit. Cautiously he peered around the trunk. Nothing but the silent coffers. He heaved a sigh of relief; he'd lost her.

But on turning back, August screamed again (and, I'm afraid to say, *again*), finding the glistening eyeball merely inches from his nose, and beyond it the delighted face of his unusual new admirer.

She retreated a little, with a regretful expression, as if she

hadn't meant to scare him. August pulled himself together and stood, dusting off his pants. He contemplated the girl, wondering what to do next, and realized there was something pitiful about her. She had the air not of some violent monster, but of a lost puppy. August felt a wave of sympathy for this strange creature.

"Your name," he said, "is Claudette, right?"

The girl nodded enthusiastically, clods of dirt dropping from her hair, and again she emitted that wet, whispering sound. It was almost as if she was attempting to communicate.

Curiously, the noise seemed to come only partly from the child. Some—*other*—layer of her voice came from a different place, the same place as the half-remembered echo he'd "heard" on his first foray into the cemetery. It was as if the sound came, August realized, from somewhere inside *himself.*

It was an unsettling sensation.

"Look, Claudette," August explained as kindly as he could under the circumstances. "You can't come with me. My aunt Hydrangea is a highly nervous person. One little butterfly sends her into a shrieking panic. So I'm pretty sure she would not react well to an unexpected visit from some little dead girl."

Claudette blinked.

"I think it's best," said August, wincing sympathetically, "if you return to . . . um . . . wherever it is you came from."

The girl moved forward with a hopeful look. The eyeball was pressed against August's chest.

The boy grimaced and sighed. He took the eyeball. Now, you've probably never handled another person's eyeball. *I* certainly haven't. But I'm sure we can both imagine how they might feel . . . perfectly awful!

"I'm sorry about this, Claudette," said August with a resigned sigh.

He swung back his arm and hurled the thing with all his might—*plunk!*—into the dark, swirling river.

CHAPTER 20

THE DUPONT TREASURE

The table in Locust Hole's dining room was composed of a closet door supported by two large pepper-curing barrels. The house, after all, was so devoid of contents that closets— never mind their doors—were scarcely necessary.

August and Hydrangea sat at either end of this makeshift table. From the ceiling hung a naked bulb concealed by a plastic bucket that served as a chandelier. The room was currently illuminated, however, by the jittery light of a single candle in a jelly jar.

"Our circumstances may be reduced," Aunt Hydrangea would say, "but that does not mean we must dine like barbarians!"

And indeed, the forks may have been plastic, the dishes mismatched, and the napkins formed from ripped-up petticoats, but the table was always laid formally, as if the governor himself were expected for dinner.

"The catfish soup," said August reassuringly, lifting his spoon to his mouth, "is delicious!"

"I'm sorry there's no sausage, sugar," sighed his aunt. "I'm afraid the loss of so much hot sauce diminished our weekly expenses." She waggled a finger at her nephew. "But I'll fix you a cream cheese cake for your birthday. I promise!"

"That's all right, ma'am," August insisted, smiling. "I'm not that hungry."

"No doubt," muttered Hydrangea bitterly. "It's all well and good, I suppose, if you can afford to dine every day on towers of pralines and crustless sandwiches."

August shot his aunt an admonishing look, though it had little effect; she was still simmering with resentment at the report of her sister's opulent circumstances.

"So," she said, dabbing the corner of her mouth with a napkin, "you say that Orchid is in good health, lives in constant mourning, and has two children. Twins. How . . . ghoulish."

"They were nice to *me*," protested August quietly. "Well, one of them was."

Hydrangea grunted, then sipped her soup.

"And your journey," she asked cautiously, attempting to appear calm, "was unremarkable? No giant alligators or other dangerous encounters?"

August observed his aunt's fluttery eyelids, and the soup spilling from her trembling spoon. Should he tell her? Surely the tale of his bizarre graveyard experience would shatter Hydrangea's frayed nerves completely. As it was, his failure to immediately answer her clearly rattled the lady.

"August?" she said sharply. "Is there something I should know?" Her agitation gathered momentum. "Did something happen? I knew catastrophe must follow this foolhardy scheme. Your first adventure abroad must surely be your last!"

"No!" cried August. Then more calmly, "No, ma'am. There was no alligator. Everything was perfectly safe and uneventful." He needed to steer Hydrangea away from this topic, to distract her before she succumbed to her fears and his newfound freedom was endangered.

"Have you ever heard," he said, abruptly but casually shifting gears, "of Orfeo DuPont's famous fossil?" He attempted to appear innocently curious.

Hydrangea looked up with a puzzled frown.

"Now, how in heaven would you hear about . . ." Her eyebrows rose in sudden revelation. *"Orchid!"* she said, like a cat coughing up a hair ball. Hydrangea shook her head in disgusted disbelief. "As if deserting us for our enemies was not enough! Now she assuredly plots to get her greedy hands on the DuPont treasure!"

August squinted.

"Treasure?"

"Great-Uncle Orfeo's hunk of Cadaverite," muttered Hydrangea, clearly preoccupied by thoughts of her sister's wickedness. "It's the rarest of gemstones, you know. Very troublesome to find. A specimen that size, the size of Orfeo's? Why, it must be worth a king's ransom."

"But . . ." August was confused. "Aunt Orchid said the stone was of value to no one but a collector."

"Pffft!" Hydrangea smacked her hand on the table in an uncharacteristically defiant gesture.

You know how sometimes two things make a sound at exactly the same time, so you might wonder if you really heard the second thing at all? August could have sworn that as Hydrangea's palm struck the weathered wood, he heard a crash from elsewhere in the house . . . the sort of violent sound that would result from someone—or some*thing*—forcing its way through a rotted basement door. Indeed, the water in his glass was rippling, as if from some tiny earthquake.

"Did you hear . . . ," he began.

But Hydrangea was all consumed by indignation and resentment.

"Remember what I told you, August. Money and prestige. That's *all* Malveaus care for. Orchid always has to be the best, have the most." Her eyes widened with realization. "She wants

you to search for the Cadaverite on her behalf, doesn't she? *That's* what she wanted with you. That's *all* she wanted with you."

August's face fell, transformed by an expression of shock and dismay.

Hydrangea softened at the boy's reaction.

"I'm sorry, sugar," she muttered, "but I fear it's true."

The lady, however, had failed to notice that August was not looking at, or even listening to, her. He was transfixed by something just beyond his aunt's right elbow.

The dining room and parlor faced each other across the foyer. From his viewpoint, August could see something rising up through the parlor floor, or rather, climbing from the black hole that opened to the basement.

A shadowy figure, with twisted, jerky movements, was heaving itself into the room. It got a foothold, then gathered height, until it crookedly stood, still strewn with weeds and dripping river water.

It was Claudette.

CHAPTER 21

A CLAMMY OBSTACLE

From the cracked door of his room, August could hear the clatter of broken china and the shrill sounds of Hydrangea's indignation downstairs.

"That child," she was grumbling, "is as clumsy as a toad in a dollhouse! The floorboards will surely smell like catfish soup for a week or more!"

August felt bad. But with few tools at his disposal, "accidentally" knocking his dinner to the floor was the only distraction he could think up at short notice. At least it had been effective. As Hydrangea squealed and fussed over the broken dish and wasted food, August had swiftly and quietly bundled Claudette upstairs . . . undetected!

He closed the door softly and turned to confront his un-invited guest.

"You smashed through a basement door?" hissed August accusingly. "I'll need to repair that in the morning, you know, before butterflies find their way in and there's explaining to be done."

But the sodden undead child was preoccupied, exploring the garret with a kind of vacant curiosity.

"You found your eyeball, I see," observed August. He was glad she had; he hadn't felt great about tossing someone else's body part into a murky river.

"Oh! No! Not that!" He darted across the room to rescue Kevin the clown from the girl's clumsily grabbing fingers.

"Not that either!" She was attempting to devour an empty Mudd Pie wrapper.

"Or that!" August retrieved his desk lamp as Claudette, with apparent fascination, followed its wire to the plug and peered into the empty holes of the adjacent outlet.

August contemplated the girl with confounded frustration.

"Why me, Claudette?" he wondered aloud. "What do you want with *me*?"

The googly eyes swiveled toward him, and the girl burbled away quite chattily. But what—if anything—she was attempting to say, August could not quite decipher.

Then she casually stuck her tongue into an empty socket hole.

"Oh no . . . ," cried August, but too late.

There was a crackling flash followed by a soft explosion, like a basketball falling into a tub of talcum powder. Claudette was propelled across the room, where she crashed noisily into an old sewing machine.

"August?" came an alarmed voice from below. "What in *heaven*?"

"Everything is fine, Aunt Hydrangea!" August responded quickly from his doorway. "Just knocked over my chair."

"Are you all right?" he whispered urgently, dashing to the girl's aid. He had seen contestants on *Are You a Dummy?* perform CPR on a limbless mannequin and thought he might actually have a good shot at reviving a shark-bite victim. But in cases where the subject was already dead, any life-restoring process seemed a bit redundant.

Indeed, Claudette's eyes were spinning madly, but she seemed otherwise undamaged.

"You know," August advised her, "your tongue doesn't normally go . . ."

He froze. *Normally.* Normal. Now, *there* was a sobering thought.

August had just reassured his friend . . . his first friend . . . his

only friend . . . that everything about himself was . . . "perfectly normal." While he was perhaps not an expert, August felt pretty confident that having an undead sidekick with erratic eyes and a fondness for sticking her tongue into electrical outlets was anything other than "perfectly normal."

With a knot in his stomach and his knees growing soft, August watched the stunned creature stagger around. This clammy, bedraggled girl could be a serious problem, a real obstacle to his new friendship with Beauregard. August's new, un-lonely life could well be over before it had even properly begun.

"If I climbed a tree," pondered August, "and just waited, she would surely wander off eventually." He pursed his lips. "But she knows where I live." His brow furrowed in concentration. "One of those other tombs in the cemetery might have room for her. But she's already bashed her way through a marble slab, so . . ." He tapped his chin. "I could take her deep into Lost Souls' Swamp and leave here there." He grimaced. "But it's called Lost Souls' Swamp for a reason. What if I can't find my *own* way out?"

Claudette, having recovered from her electrocution, was now peering into August's large jar of Ping-Pong balls, shaking it and gurgling with what seemed like delight at the resulting sound. Suddenly, with a moist *plop!,* her wayward left eyeball fell out of her face and into the jar.

"Ugh!" said August, appalled. "You cannot stay here,

Claudette," he muttered. "We *need* to get you back where you belong."

Claudette plunged her hand into the jar and frantically swished it around. She removed a white sphere and forced it into her eye socket, consulting a broken mirror to check the results. Nope! Just a Ping-Pong ball.

She tried again.

And again.

August sighed wearily and massaged his forehead.

"We need," he repeated, nodding in self-agreement, "to talk to someone who knows a thing or two about dead folks!"

CHAPTER 22

GOODNIGHT'S FUNERAL PARLOR

On the south side of town, Pepperville's Main Street was residential, lined by grand old townhomes and grander, older oak trees draped with Spanish moss. August and Claudette arrived in the tranquil, leafy neighborhood early enough that it still lay shrouded in cool morning mist.

Slender fluted lampposts lined the median in the center of the road, each sporting two golden orbs that hovered in the air, insubstantial and blurred by the fog. To August, who had never seen one, the illuminated street had a wistful magic, like the Christmas tree in Stella Starz's living room . . . before her impossible cat Officer Claw had scaled it in pursuit of the feathery fairy at the top.

"I hope you weren't too uncomfortable," said August

absently, studying his map in the weak light, "sleeping under my bed all night." He looked up with a sudden thought. "*Do* you sleep? Whatever the case," he mused, "I suppose the floor could not have been worse than a stone sarcophagus."

They arrived at a garden path that crossed a lawn and led to an imposing villa. Lush potted palms flanked the semicircular portico, and the tall, pointed gables were clad in decorative, scalloped shingles. But even through the mist, one could see the place had a shabby air and was in want of a fresh coat of paint.

Claudette ogled a wooden sign mounted on a post by the sidewalk. August wasn't sure if she could read it. But if she could have, the undead girl would have understood that the pair had arrived at "Goodnight's Funeral Parlor."

* * *

The interior was almost as lightless as Locust Hole. The effect, however, was rich, rather than gloomy. The walls, columns, arches, and heavy turned banisters were all carved from lustrous, reddish-brown rosewood, and the place smelled distinctly of lemon-scented furniture polish.

The only sounds were the innocuous hum of a vending machine in the corner of the foyer, and the faint strains of organ music drifting from speakers recessed into the ceiling.

There was no one around. At the foot of a wide, twisting staircase sat a huge leather-topped desk, vacant but for a sleeping computer monitor on one side and a tarnished service bell on the other.

August let his palm fall on the dome-shaped device, and it rang clearly and cleanly, echoing through the large, heavily paneled space.

Nothing.

He tried again, waiting several moments for a response.

"Hello?" he called, mounting the lowest stair and peering upward.

Dusty silence.

"I don't think . . ." He turned to Claudette.

But Claudette was gone.

"Claudette?" August spun in a circle. He darted back through the swinging front door and checked outside. She wasn't there.

Returning to the desk, his eyes searching every darkened corner, August noticed tall double doors at one end of the foyer that led to some other space. Cautiously he went to explore.

The room he found had once been a rather grand parlor. A bruise-colored marble mantel faced the entrance, bearing large stone urns filled with plastic flowers. The boy's dim reflection shifted in mottled mirrored tiles that encased the chimney breast.

The parlor, however, no longer functioned as an elegant room for entertaining but as a showroom . . . for coffins. A large, aging cardboard sign on an easel read "Peruvian flu got you down? Take a dirt nap in a Goodnight casket."

The long wooden cases displayed a wide range of finishes, from the blackest ebony to the palest maple, and their polished fittings and rails gleamed sumptuously in the dim light. Some were displayed along the walls, on discreet steel frames that suspended one above another. Others were placed in a circular arrangement around the room, like the numbers of a clock, elevated at one end so they tilted forward for convenient viewing.

At the very center, raised on its own festooned plinth, rested a casket of snowy-white lacquer. It was smaller than most; child-sized. Like many of the others, it was fitted with a split lid, the upper half being propped open, so the plush interior might be admired.

Seated inside, lounging against a creamy satin pillow with a thoroughly self-satisfied expression, was Claudette.

"What the devil are you doing?" hissed August in horror. "Get *out* of there, right now! You're not supposed—"

He was interrupted by a man's muffled voice that came from behind.

"Good morning, sir!"

August jumped around to find himself facing a plump gentleman holding an equally plump beignet in his sugary fingers. It smelled buttery and fresh and utterly delicious.

"Jupiter Goodnight," the man introduced himself, "undertaker." He mumbled rather, his mouth being full (presumably of buttery, fresh, delicious beignet).

His attire, a handsomely cut suit and vest, was predictably dark and somber. But by contrast, the man's face was quite jovial, wide and round, and his lips twitched constantly, as if suppressing an unwanted smile.

"How might we assist you," asked Jupiter Goodnight, beaming and staring widely at August's helmet, "in conveying your departed one to the Other Side?"

"Well, um," stammered August. He paused, searching for the right words, couldn't find them, so jumped right in. "I was wondering if . . ."

"Speak up, sir, if you will."

". . . wondering if you might explain the procedure for cases where your departed one . . . eh . . . comes *back*!"

"Comes *back*?" declared Goodnight, stifling a giggle. August felt a giggle coming on too, and wondered at the man's mirthful demeanor, which seemed entirely at odds with his doleful profession.

"Oh, at Goodnight's, sir, death is generally a one-way affair. We pride ourselves on never having had a repeat customer!"

August bit his lower lip.

"Well, Mr. Goodnight," he said, half-apologetic, half-boastful, "I believe I may have your very first." August threw his arm and hand out in a *"ta-da!"* gesture, and spun back to the showroom.

Claudette was nowhere to be seen.

August glanced back at Jupiter Goodnight. The undertaker's lips were twitching merrily, but his eyebrows rose in baffled expectation.

"Claudette?" hissed August. "Where are you?"

Suddenly, with a gleeful grin, Claudette bolted upright in her coffin, where she had been lying concealed.

And for the second time that week, August observed a grown adult crumple to the floor in an old-fashioned swoon.

* * *

"Mr. Goodnight?" whispered August, gently patting the man's ample cheek. "Are you all right?"

The well-fed undertaker sat on the floor, legs splayed, propped against a burled maple casket with silver handles. His eyelids fluttered and slowly opened.

"You fainted clean away, sir," explained August gently.

"Fainted clean away?" The man was fuzzy-headed. But then he caught sight of the hovering Claudette, and with a start, his wits returned.

"Little dead girls have *no* business running around scaring folks half to death!" he protested, wagging his finger at Claudette. "Popping up out of coffins like some Halloween jack-in-the-box!" His animated, mirthful lips made it impossible to determine how dismayed the gentleman truly was.

"This sort of thing," Goodnight continued, "is bad for

business. Very bad indeed. In these parts, at least, folks prefer their dearly departed to stay that way!"

"I can see why," agreed August enthusiastically. "The unexpected arrival of an undead visitor can be very . . . inconvenient. I can tell you that it is so for me."

He fixed the undertaker with an injured expression.

"Can Goodnight's Funeral Parlor," said August, deadly serious, "help me to return this girl to . . . well, wherever it is she came from?"

"Goodnight's handles only the *dead,* sir," said the undertaker, "not the *undead*!" He took a large bite of the beignet that remarkably remained in his grip. The distressing incident had left him, it seemed, quite hungry.

"You need to find yourself," he mumbled, "someone who knows a thing or two about magic." He gulped, then licked his lips. "You need to find yourself a sorcerer, perhaps, or conjure man . . . or at least a ball gazer."

He looked at Claudette and shook the last of the beignet in her direction.

"Because what you've got yourself here, sir . . . is a zombie!"

CHAPTER 23

A SMALL AND ICY HAND

North of the Pelican State Bank, Pepperville's Main Street became increasingly commercial, the smart gardens and villas giving way to a jumble of stores, restaurants, and traffic.

Locust Hole lay downriver, so August and Claudette had entered town from the tranquil, residential south side. Downtown Pepperville presented August with an entirely new, and alien, environment.

In reality, it was a small town on a sleepy bend in the river. But to a boy who had been cloistered for his entire existence, Pepperville felt clamorous and chaotic. The landscape of brick, stucco, and asphalt added a glaring harshness to the already stifling heat. The buildings felt narrow and tightly crammed together. The passing cars were deafening, and the smell of their exhaust made August light-headed.

And the people! *So* many people! It seemed that every minute or two, August was yanking Claudette out of the path of another pedestrian (which obviously doesn't represent that many people at all, but you get the point). Their progress was further hampered by numerous wooden posts supporting the two-story galleries that fronted many buildings, resulting in much dodging and weaving and declarations of "oops!" and "sorry!" and "excuse me!"

While attempting to prevent his lurching companion from colliding into other people and things, August was scanning the shop signs on either side of Main Street.

"Flowers by Fleur," he read aloud. "Jean-Claude's Cafeteria. Cinema Athénaïs. Black River Tattoo."

But there was no advertisement for services involving sorcery or ball gazing.

"Hold up a minute!" said August, stopping so abruptly that he earned the grunting protest of a passerby. "Madame Marvell! What is it that her sign reads?" He frowned, rooting around his memory. "Yes, that's it: Ball Gazing, Magic, and More."

He grabbed the zombie's arm, his eyebrows high.

"Let's get home, Claudette," he said with excitement. "We need to pay a call upon a certain wild child!"

They turned back toward Locust Hole, but before taking a

step, August was startled by a sudden hammering quite close to his ear.

To his left was a large store window and, arching across the glass, painted lettering in a familiar font read "Grosbeak's General Store & Soda Shop."

Beyond the signage, flattened against the window, was a pink palm. Beyond that was the face of Beauregard Malveau. And beyond *that,* seated merely feet away, were Beauregard's companions: Gaston, Langley, and Belladonna. Their table sported festive-looking root beer floats, although only three, for Belladonna was cradling a tiny but serious-looking coffee cup, and scowling.

"Cousin August!" Beauregard's voice was muffled by the thick layer of glass. "Come, join us!" He made an invitational gesture.

For a split second, August felt a surge of delight. Stella Starz and her friends also frequented a restaurant, where they would dissect the unlikely events of the episode, effortlessly wielding exotic-looking foodstuffs with chopsticks. Grosbeak's interior was cluttered and poorly lit, entirely dissimilar to the airy, bamboo modernity of Sushi Yum-Yum. But the sociable, table-based gathering was thrillingly familiar.

August's glee, however, lasted only for as long as it took for him to recall the zombie at his side. He glanced at Claudette and succumbed to a wave of panic and despair.

They could not meet her. They must not know her. They should certainly never associate him with this . . . this *creature*.

August shook his head vigorously at Beauregard, then pointed at his wristwatch.

"Running late!" he mouthed silently at the window. This was a device that Stella regularly employed to avoid interaction with her father's disagreeable girlfriend, Hedwig.

"Just for a minute!" responded Beauregard. "Bring your friend!" Then, half coaxing, half pleading and with an irresistible grin, he said, "Why, come *on*!"

August could not simply walk away. To do so, at this point, would have been actively rude. He flapped his arms helplessly and headed inside.

"Remember to speak up," he muttered to himself. "And you!" he said to Claudette. "Keep that eyeball in its socket!"

* * *

To the left of the front door was the small general store, sacks of dried beans and flour slumping on the floor; canned, jarred, and packaged goods cramming the shelves all the way to the ceiling. Somewhere high up, well out of his reach, August spotted the familiar navy-and-yellow packaging of his favorite treat.

To the right of the door was the small, weary-looking soda shop. Swivel stools of spotted chrome with cracked pink vinyl seats ran the length of the counter while a handful of Formica-topped tables and peppermint-green metal chairs were clustered near the large window.

A saggy-eyed elderly man with a red bow tie and thin wisps of hair protruding from his rimless cap was tugging weakly on the lever of a shiny silver tap, one of several behind the counter. On catching sight of the newcomers, his mouth opened slightly, and he stared until the sarsaparilla spilled over his fingers, demanding his attention.

As Beauregard commandeered two more chairs, dragging them across the faded black-and-white linoleum tiles, August removed his helmet.

"It's for the butterflies," he explained meekly, pressing Claudette into one chair and settling himself in the other.

"You've met Gaston," said Beauregard, still standing. The well-fed delivery boy nodded his ginger head. "And Langley." The tall boy touched the brim of his hat. "And my sister, of course." Belladonna glared over the lip of her cup.

August smiled, acknowledging the assembly.

But no one was looking at August. August and his helmet and his butterflies were apparently old news. Rather, their disconcerted gazes were fixed upon Claudette.

No one spoke.

"Beauregard Malveau," announced Beauregard suddenly, as

if abruptly remembering his manners, "of Château Malveau." He leaned with an outstretched hand toward Claudette, who stared at it blankly, until a nudge from August caused her to clumsily reach out and grasp it.

Beauregard sharply withdrew his hand with a gasp.

"She's so *cold*!" he said with mild horror.

August thought quickly.

"C-C-Claudette . . . ," he stammered, "is . . . um . . . an exchange student. From Lapland."

Stella Starz had once rescued an unwitting Laplander from making a catastrophic choice in the lunch line (the mac and cheese was notorious for resulting in bad breath and occasional diarrhea). The grateful exchange student had gifted Stella with a reindeer, the concealment of which had made for a particularly hilarious episode.

"She just moved here."

"Looks like Claudette had a pretty rough journey," chuckled Langley, glancing with amusement at the others.

Claudette's eyes loosely swiveled to the lanky youth, and Langley's jaw dropped as, from the root beer float in front of him, the girl casually plucked the long-handled spoon and popped it into her own mouth.

"Hey!" protested Langley. "That's my . . ."

He was interrupted by the grotesque sucking and slurping that ensued. Five pairs of eyes bulged as the spoon handle

disappeared further and further into Claudette's face, until, with a loud gulp, it was entirely gone.

For a moment, there was utter silence, until Beauregard collected himself and delivered a broad—if forced—smile.

"In these parts," he said, "we welcome all strangers . . . and . . . eh, their . . . *customs?*" He glanced encouragingly at Claudette, then frowned at his friends, kicking one of Langley's boots beneath the table. "Don't we, guys?"

Langley and Gaston nodded in obedient agreement.

"Ha!" barked Belladonna, and without further explanation removed herself from the table and the establishment.

"Claudette," continued Beauregard, entirely ignoring his sister's dramatic exit, "*must* attend the crawfish boil at Château Malveau."

"Oh, no!" blurted August, so abruptly that Beauregard blinked with surprise. "I mean, thank you, of course, but . . . um . . . I don't think that's Claudette's sort of thing."

August glanced at the girl and gulped, his mind working furiously.

"She's unused to crowds, you see, having lived mostly on the frozen tundra. With reindeer."

"Nonsense!" cried Beauregard, now fully recovered and his usual jovial self. "Who doesn't love a party? We'll give this chilly Lapp a warm Pepperville welcome, won't we, guys?" He gave Gaston a hearty slap on the back.

"What?" said a startled Gaston. "Why, yes. Sure. Pepperville welcome."

Beauregard looked August square in the face, grinning from ear to ear.

"We'll see you both there tomorrow." He leaned over and gripped August's wrist. "I absolutely, positively insist!"

CHAPTER 24

MADAME MARVELL

The bank beneath Locust Hole's gazebo had, over time, slumped into the canal, taking the steps with it. August and Claudette stood inside the open-sided structure, merely inches above the lapping waves that cast shimmering, dancing ripples across the ceiling. Once the shaded, breezy site of summer pleasures, the gazebo had fallen into sorry disrepair, its posts crooked and lacy fretwork shattered. The interior echoed with the feathery flapping of wings as a curious pigeon investigated the hole in the roof.

Grabbing the rail for support, August leaned out over the water. Beneath him, a shoal of tiny minnows hovered sleepily in the protective embrace of a partially sunken canoe. The bow still protruded from the water, providing a perch for an iridescent dragonfly.

Only a few yards away, still alarmingly angled, bobbed the makeshift houseboat. From this proximity, August could see that Madame Marvell's sign was weathered, cracked, and old and most certainly predated the young resident.

"You ought to be careful," instructed a sudden voice from behind them, causing August to almost lose his grip and plunge into the canal. "There's a giant alligator prowling these parts, so folks are saying."

The wild child herself was perched on the gazebo's rear rail, hugging a post for balance. With her free arm, she was clutching the familiar plastic colander, which was half filled with plump slime-colored frogs, gently croaking and clambering over one another.

The girl had a pert little nose; small, dark eyes, bright like a squirrel's; and a ragged mop of tow-colored hair that had clearly not seen a comb any time recently. Her limbs were skinny but looked strong and well designed for clambering in trees.

"Have you seen it?" asked August. "The alligator?"

"I've seen *something*," responded the girl, "deep in the water. Huge and white. I reckon that must have been it."

She leaped lightly to the floor.

"You're the boy who lives in the roof of that ramshackle old house," she informed August. "Don't look so surprised; you think you're the only person who owns a telescope?"

August flushed. She had been observing him, just as he had been observing her.

"Folks in town," the girl continued with her head tilted, "say that you're a ghost. But I've never known a ghost who needs a helmet to protect himself from bees."

"Butterflies, actually," mumbled August, prompting a dubious look in return. And then quickly, to change the subject, he said, "Are you Madame Marvell?"

The girl twisted her lips and looked at her toes.

"Kind of," she said. "I had another name once, I think. But I forget it." She swung her hips from side to side in a childish manner. "The first Madame Marvell was my grandmother. She up and died a long time back. I reckon she wouldn't mind me borrowing her name."

"You live *alone*?" August was shocked.

Madame Marvell shrugged and nodded, like it was a thing of little significance.

"But *not*," she added, fixing August with a stern look, "if Child Services comes asking. You understand?" She took a step forward and poked her index finger into August's ribs. For a little thing, she was quite intimidating (which, when you think about it, isn't actually that uncommon: possums . . . hungry babies . . . bad-tempered poodles . . .).

"If the folks from the county come around, you tell them that my mawmaw's fetching groceries at Grosbeak's. I'm nearly ten years old. I can look out for myself. Got it?"

August got it. He nodded dutifully.

"Hey!" objected Madame Marvell. "Stop that!" She defensively switched her colander to the opposite hip. "Can you tell your zombie to leave my frogs alone?"

August was flabbergasted.

"H-H-How . . . ," he stammered. "I mean . . . you know she's a *zombie*? How . . ."

"She's licking my frogs," said Madame Marvell, like it was the most obvious thing in the world. "Her eyes are all googly, and she looks like she just dug her way out of the grave. What else is she going to be?"

"Have you met many zombies before?"

"None at all," admitted Madame Marvell. "But my mawmaw knew a bit about magic, and I'm familiar with the concept."

"Concept!" repeated August, impressed. "Do *you* know anything about magic?"

"Not a whole lot. My mawmaw taught me a thing or two."

August went on to explain his predicament and to express

his pressing desire to return Claudette to wherever it was that she came from.

Madame Marvell listened, considered, then nodded toward the canal.

"I'm not sure how I can help," she said. "But you best come aboard."

CHAPTER 25

THE ZOMBIE STONE

The houseboat's interior was overly warm, small, and as you might imagine, far from even-keeled. August purposely lingered at the front end of the "cabin," for fear that any more weight added to the stern might cause the listing craft to finally slide, casually and silently backward, with merely a bubble or two, into the murky water.

On the starboard wall, the wall facing August's bedroom window, stood his old friend, the mustard-colored television. Beside this, a gas-powered camping stove and empty frying pan sat upon a dented mini icebox. Opposite, a mere three feet away, a weary tweed sofa lay somewhere beneath a mess of blankets and pillows.

At the far end, the end where any runaway Ping-Pong balls

or marbles would certainly have gathered, a table was cluttered with a jumble of seemingly random objects: a large rusted iron key, hard candies wrapped in foil, strings of iridescent beads, and purple candles. At the center of this colorful hodgepodge sat the crudely fashioned cloth doll that August had often seen seated beside Madame Marvell on deck.

But the most arresting feature of this floating home was its walls, which were entirely concealed behind a collection of posters, postcards, playbills, and programs, all featuring the acts of illusionists, magicians, and wizards. The material was of varying age and condition and had obviously been amassed over many years.

"Don't most people," said August, gazing around, "pin up pictures of athletes or actors or musicians?"

Stella Starz had many oversized images of her idol, the one-eyed xylophonist Yuko Yukiyama, on her bedroom walls. Yukiyama was celebrated almost as much for her creative and glamorous eye patches as she was for her extraordinary percussion skills.

"They're not mine," said Madame Marvell, pumping a foot pedal beneath a steel sink and washing her hands in the resulting stream of water. August would have washed his hands too, if he'd been handling frogs. The amphibious creatures had been left outside in their colander, and August wondered if they'd still be there when the girl went to retrieve them.

"My mawmaw, she dabbled in magic, like I told you." The girl grabbed a towel. "And when you're keen about a thing, you admire the folks that do it real well, right? Like ballplayers, or singers, or race car drivers." She joined August in gazing up at the fading images of theatrical performers long dead.

"But my mawmaw's heroes were all conjurers and whatnot, especially those with distinguished magic skills."

"Hey!" exclaimed August suddenly. "I know that man." He moved toward the wall, and lifted his helmet net to peer more closely. "I believe we're related."

The poster was certainly among the oldest, for its once rich colors were faint and dull, and much of it was papered over with later additions to the collection. August wasn't sure if the artwork was the product of photography or illustration or something in between.

In any event, it depicted a familiar, mustachioed man with a tasseled hat and unusually large, round eyeglasses that magnified eyes of the palest gold, like late-summer marsh grass.

This was a much larger picture than that on the playbill in Orchid's tea table. In this image, Orfeo DuPont's full figure was easily accommodated, and his gesture was courteous and attentive, as if inviting the viewer into the poster itself.

From the skull-shaped fossil in his wand, a mysterious green vapor rose and swirled around several richly costumed figures in the background. And it was these who provided the most absorbing aspect of the scene.

The men, women, and one child struck mannered poses that were reminiscent of an elegant dance, but simultaneously unnatural, stiff, and unsettling. The angular, awkward postures reminded August of Claudette. And indeed, the "dancers" were similarly cadaverous and ragged, as if freshly disentombed.

They were zombies.

But unlike August's undead admirer, the eyes of these zombies were glazed over, glowing with a milky light, as if deeply entranced.

" 'DuPont's Dance of the Dead,' " said August, reading the bold and decorative typeface above the picture. " 'The world's premier necromancer employs the Zombie Stone to reanimate the deceased for your diversion and delight.' "

"Orfeo DuPont," exclaimed Madame Marvell, incredulous, "was your kin?"

August nodded absently, still transfixed by the haunting tableau. The girl looked at the poster, then at August, then back at the poster. "There is some resemblance," she admitted.

"So I'm told," muttered August. "What's a necromancer?"

"A kind of sorcerer," explained Madame Marvell. "Necromancy is magic to do with the dead. Most of the time we live in our world, and the dead, they live in their own, and that's that.

But necromancers, they use a Go-Between to access the other world, the world of the dead, and maybe even talk to the spirit folks that live there."

"Go-Between?"

"It's . . ." Madame Marvell looked upward, thinking. "It's an enchanted sort of thing that works like a window, I guess, or a bridge, between the two places. It doesn't *look* like a window or a bridge, of course."

She moved to the cluttered table and lifted the rag doll seated there. The thing was coarsely stitched together from old sack-cloth, flat-faced and bald, with buttons for eyes and stitches for a mouth. Its only garment was a frayed scrap of patterned silk, worn like a scarf and pinned at the chest with a flower-shaped brooch of lilac stones.

"Delfine here, for example," said Madame Marvell, shaking the doll so its limbs waggled, "is a Go-Between. She helps me talk to my mawmaw."

"Your . . . dead grandmother?"

"Why, sure. This is mawmaw's best pin: real amethyst. It acts like a kind of magnet, draws her spirit toward it. I light some candles too: purple, her favorite color. It all helps mawmaw find Delfine, and then me, so I can ask her questions when I need help. Or sometimes we just visit, you know?"

"And you actually hear her voice?"

"Mmm. Not *exactly*. Not like I hear your voice right now.

It kind of comes from somewhere else . . . somewhere maybe, inside *me*."

A shiver ran up the back of August's neck. He thought of the voice he'd sort of, somehow heard in the cemetery. Claudette's voice.

"But Delfine's just a homemade," continued Madame Marvell, propping the limp doll against the pitcher filled with wild iris. "She's stuffed with herbs and spells, and she works fine, I reckon. But *some* Go-Betweens were created with ancient magic by powerful mages over the sea, and they're far more powerful. Like the Zombie Stone."

"What *is* the Zombie Stone?"

"It's what made your ancestor so famous," said Madame Marvell, stretching upward and tapping the hunk of rock on Orfeo's staff.

"You mean the DuPont treasure? The Cadaverite?"

"I never heard of any DuPont treasure," confessed Madame Marvell. "Or cadav . . . cadav *what*? But everyone knows about Orfeo's Zombie Stone. See, it says it right here on the poster: 'The world's premier necromancer employs the Zombie Stone to reanimate the deceased.'"

She leaned in conspiratorially. August and Claudette did so too.

"They say," she whispered, glancing over her shoulder, as if some dark force might be listening, "its magic was so strong that

Orfeo used it to draw spirits from the other world right back into this one. They'd arrive all lost and confused, so they'd slip right back into the unfortunate, moldy bodies they had left behind, and become, well . . ." She nodded pointedly at Claudette.

"Orfeo made his zombies dance about like fools, poor creatures, just to show off. Or perhaps for money. Or both."

All three gazed up at the poster in somber reflection.

"So . . ." The wheels of August's mind were turning. "If the Zombie Stone could suck a ghost, or spirit, into this world and force it back into its corpse"—his eyes glided sideways toward Claudette—"could it work in reverse? Could it drive the spirit back to the beyond, and *unmake* a zombie?"

Madame Marvell considered the undead girl drooling in her houseboat. She looked at August and shrugged.

"I'm not sure," she admitted. "But I don't see why not."

CHAPTER 26

THE NECROMANCER'S SISTER

August poured tea into a cup and uncapped the bottle of bourbon.

"But I told you, sugar," protested Hydrangea, "I'm in no particular need of fortified tea."

"Um ... I think," responded August, wincing, "you'll be wanting a cup of it very shortly. We have a small problem."

He glanced nervously over his shoulder, down the hallway.

"A small *zombie* problem."

"Zombie?" repeated his aunt, mystified.

"Now, Aunt Hydrangea, please try to remain calm. I promise that she's perfectly harmless."

"*She? Harm*less? August, what in heaven are you talking about?"

August turned and gestured toward someone beyond Hydrangea's line of sight. The lady's eyes bulged at the sound of heavy, uneven, dragging footsteps. As they progressed along the hallway toward the parlor, Hydrangea stood up swiftly and turned to August in alarm.

August had done his best to clean Claudette up a bit, wiping off her face and combing most of the debris from her hair. But her appearance was still, at best, disconcerting, and upon seeing her, Hydrangea reacted as you might expect: she clutched the back of the fainting couch, stifled a scream in her handkerchief, and looked set to swoon.

Until something surprising happened.

August watched as his aunt's expression of horror morphed into something else, something utterly unexpected: recognition.

"Why, color me amazed," said Hydrangea, peering at Claudette with disbelief. "It can't be." The gripped handkerchief fell to her side, and she took a step forward.

"Claudette DuPont?"

* * *

Hydrangea fetched one of the family photographs that lingered on the mantel, propped behind the headless goatherd clock. She smiled nervously as Claudette sat heavily beside her on the fainting couch. August approached from behind, peering over his aunt's shoulder.

"There she is," said Hydrangea, pointing.

The mildewed, antique image was of the sort that was photographed in black-and-white, then colored by hand. Beneath it, in ambitious lettering, was displayed the name of the studio where it had been created: "Photography by Fontaine. New Madrid."

The portrait depicted two children. The girl, who stood holding a kitten, was clearly Claudette. The photograph could not have been taken very long before she died, for her height appeared much the same. It was strange to see her looking rosy-cheeked, neatly dressed, and generally rather pretty.

The other child was a boy, around August's age, seated. His piercing pale gold eyes were unusually large and round, rendered larger by large, round glasses. In his lap he held a specimen jar, inside of which rested a skull-shaped fossil.

"Is that . . ." August was incredulous. "Is that *Orfeo DuPont* as a boy?"

Hydrangea nodded.

"You favor him, August!"

It was true. The resemblance between August and the grown-up Orfeo was certainly of note. But August was, after all, just a boy, many years from twirled mustaches and an adult frame. The similarity between the DuPont boys at the same age was *remarkable.*

"She thinks I'm *him,*" said August in quiet revelation. "*That's* why she's following me around. She thinks I'm her brother!"

As if to confirm this theory, Claudette beamed up at him with a grin of devotion.

"Great-Aunt Claudette," said Hydrangea with some pride, "is a family legend." She patted the zombie's arm. "Only nine years of age, when she just up and drowned in the canal. They say she jumped from the gazebo roof. Or fell. Although why she might have been up there in the first place, no one has ever known. Such a tragedy." She offered Claudette a sympathetic smile.

"What about *my* tragedy?" cried August, striding around the couch to face his aunt. "I just started to make friends. To have a life of my own. But now *this*"—he flapped his hand at Claudette—"is ruining everything!"

He stuffed his hands in his pockets and got a little pouty.

"Beauregard already thinks I'm peculiar. Now I've got some zombie following me around because she thinks I'm her dead brother! And now you tell me that she's a DuPont? That in fact we *are* related? That this raggedy, rotting thing is my great-great-aunt, or whatever?"

Claudette grunted and gazed dolefully down at her tattered dress.

"Sorry, Claudette," muttered August, with some level of apology, "but you've been dead for a long time. It's not pretty."

August swiftly dropped to one knee and grabbed his aunt's wrist.

"Aunt Hydrangea," he said urgently. "Were you aware that the DuPont treasure is also known as the Zombie Stone?"

"Why, everyone knows *that,* sugar," responded Hydrangea, as if August were the only person in the world who didn't. "It's how Orfeo acquired his zombies for that wretched act of his. What was it again? The Dancers of Death, or some such dreadful thing?"

"You didn't think to mention it?" cried August.

"How was I to know," Hydrangea bristled defensively, "that you had a small zombie problem?"

August bit his lip and lowered his eyes. He listened to his breath for a moment and quieted his frustration.

"Aunt," he said again, with kind, controlled calmness, "I need to return Claudette's spirit to the world it belongs in. The other world, where the dead reside. Preferably by tomorrow," he added, mindful of the crawfish boil at Château Malveau.

He stood.

"In order to do so, I have to find the Zombie Stone. Do you have *any* idea where it might be, or what happened to it?"

Hydrangea opened her mouth and shrugged helplessly.

"It's for *me,* ma'am"—August fixed her gaze intently—"not your sister."

"I mean . . ." The lady shook her head, racking her brains. "Uncle Orfeo was a bit of a spendthrift, sugar. I'm afraid we've had a few of those in the family."

"Aunt Orchid told me," said August. "She said that our circumstances . . ."

"Orfeo," Hydrangea interrupted with a glower, "sold off many DuPont heirlooms to pay his debts, including most of the antique family jewels and gems. I'd be very surprised if the Cadaverite was not among them. It would have fetched a handsome sum, I'm certain of it."

"Do you know who might have bought them?"

Hydrangea shook her head.

"It all happened, oh my, long before I was born." She paused, had a thought. "But I could swear there's a stack of old bills and receipts hanging around the house somewhere. Perhaps there would be some record of the sale in those. They were in a cupboard, I believe . . . or no, perhaps a bureau. Now, where *is* that old desk?"

She thoughtfully tapped the glass protecting the photograph.

"It had one short leg, as I recall, and had to be propped up with books."

CHAPTER 27

THE TATTOOED GEMOLOGIST

"It's the correct address." August looked up at the shop front, then down at the receipt in his hands. "But Black River Tattoo," he observed to Claudette, "doesn't sound much like a jewelry store."

The boutique's interior was compact, a feature enhanced by the entire place being painted dark purple and by the presence of an enormous, bushy-bearded man who consumed much of the available space.

He was perched upon a reclining seat, not unlike a dentist's chair, and brow furrowed, he was applying a buzzing pen-like device to his own (already heavily tattooed) forearm. His head was slightly narrower than his giant neck, and his flat nose had the air of one that had been broken more than once.

A limp, poorly postured young woman stood nearby. She had pink dreadlocks that hung in all directions from the top of her head, even over her face, and her scrawny knees poked through ripped stockings. She was perusing the many framed pictures that smothered the walls, which, on closer inspection, were revealed to represent a vast catalog of tattoo designs.

"What do you reckon, Buford?" the young woman was saying as August and Claudette entered the store. "A crow? No, a scorpion!" She tilted her head, examining her options. "I know! How about a giant white alligator, like the one everyone's been talking—"

She abruptly stopped midsentence upon spotting the newcomers. Beneath the ring dangling from her nose, an awestruck smile spread across her black-painted lips.

"Well, check out the little Goth," she said with unchecked admiration. "That is an awesome look, girl! How'd you come by that sickly pallor? You look deader than a pork chop! I just love the dark eye circles. And are those"—she moved in to examine Claudette's arm more closely—"oh, so cool: stitches?!"

Claudette lifted her hand to cover a sort of gurgling, simpering giggle.

"Good afternoon," said August, nudging the zombie into silence and removing his helmet. "We're looking for Juneau's Jewel Box."

"Gone, bro!" said the huge, bearded man without looking up. "Years ago." He spoke in a kind of high-pitched, husky wheeze, almost as if he'd run out of voice. "It was my pawpaw's place. We Juneaus have been jewelers for generations. The old coot gave me the business after he came down with that Peruvian flu; knew he was done for, I reckon."

His eyes swiveled upward to engage August, although his head remained unmoved.

"And I tried to keep the place going. Really, I did. *Honest!*"

August wasn't sure why *he* should warrant such an apologetic explanation.

"Even got myself a degree in gemology, I did." Buford sat up now and, turning off the tattoo machine, placed it on an adjacent steel cabinet. "But I'm an artist, bro. Got to create. The ink, it's in my blood; you know?"

August didn't know in the least, but he nodded sympathetically.

"We still got some nice swag, though," wheezed Buford Juneau, standing up so that his flat wool cap was merely inches from the ceiling.

He beckoned, and obediently August followed him to the back of the store, where beneath a row of horned cattle skulls, the cash register sat on a display case. Under the glass, resting on black velvet, was an exhibit of very particular jewelry: rings, pendants, and bracelets of silver, ornately cast in the shape of serpents, bats, and other grotesque designs. Some were set with colored gems that formed the eyes of dragons or were gripped in the talons of some disembodied monster.

"How about a little something in green," suggested Buford brightly, "to complement the young lady's complexion?"

August spread out the receipt that he'd found, as Hydrangea had suggested he might, stuffed in a drawer of his desk. It was obviously very old, one corner torn away altogether. At the top was a business letterhead, that of Juneau's Jewel Box. Below, the paper was printed with faint green horizontal lines. Vertical lines of faded red and blue formed columns at left and right. The itemized entries were handwritten. The ink was faded but mostly legible.

"Actually," said August, pointing at the document, "this family heirloom was sold to Juneau's many years ago." He gazed up at the tattooed gemologist. "I was wondering if you still have records of what happened to it . . . of who bought it from you."

Buford unearthed a pair of glasses from his pocket. They had unexpected, bright blue frames.

" 'Raw Cadaverite. C and P,' " he read, peering down at August's fingertip. " 'One hundred thirty-five dollars.' "

He straightened, rubbed his palms on his thighs, and glanced toward a narrow door in the corner. August could see, for the door was ajar, some boxes and toilet paper in the storage space beyond.

"Why, sure," mused Buford, "we got records that go way back. But we don't need those." He returned to the receipt. "We didn't buy this item from your family. See, this is the credit column. The one hundred thirty-five dollars isn't a payment from us to the customer, but from the customer to us."

August was puzzled.

"Why would someone pay *you* for their own property?"

"It's not a sale, bro. This is a charge for services rendered. C and P; that's shorthand for cut and polish—"

"Buford!" interrupted the dreadlocked young woman excitedly. "I know what I want!" She jiggled up and down, clapping her hands like a small child. "I want this girl, right here." She jerked her thumb at Claudette, who grinned sheepishly. "On my left shoulder. Can you do her?"

Buford glanced at August and rolled his eyes.

"Sure, Destiny. If that's all right with the little girl." Claudette nodded with great enthusiasm. "Take a picture with your phone, okay?"

"What's the meaning of 'cut and polish'?" asked August, tilting his head to pointedly reclaim Buford's attention.

"Well," replied Buford, scratching the scalp beneath his cap. "Says here it's raw Cadaverite, right? Means it's still in its natural state. Most gemstones are pretty rough and ugly when they first get dug out of the ground. See these raw garnets?"

Buford withdrew a small cardboard box from a drawer beneath the register and removed the lid. Inside rattled a group of brownish, pea-sized stones, scuffed and dull, not unlike common gravel.

"Pretty drab, yes? Now, cut and polished." He reached into the display case and placed a ring on the counter for August's inspection. The bauble was formed in the shape of a pair of skeleton hands. They gripped a glowing, translucent gemstone of dark and lustrous red. "Unrecognizable, right? You'd never know it was the same stone."

August stared at the ring, thinking.

"So, what," he said quietly, "would cut-and-polished *Cadaverite* look like?"

"Oh. Now, that's a rare one," mused Buford. "Don't see those often; most of them are locked up in museums, I reckon. But Cadaverite shines up to a swank sort of amber color. *Real* vivid. Lots of light refraction." He took the garnet ring and returned it to the case.

"The best, and rarest, Cadaverites have this layer of compressed carbon at the center. Shows up like a swirl of black. *Those* specimens are usually cut into a perfect sphere. Like a marble, I guess."

August's jaw fell. His mind spun.

It couldn't be.

Could it?

"A large, vivid amber marble," he repeated, "with a swirl of black at the center?"

"That's right, bro." Buford nodded. "They look so like them that in the business, they're known as alligator eyes."

CHAPTER 28

AN OVERDUE MAKEOVER

August broke the news to his aunt before breakfast the following morning.

"It was just rolling around in a dusty drawer," sputtered Hydrangea as she paced the kitchen, ruffled robe swirling, "unidentified for all these years? Why, we've been sitting on a fortune—a *fortune,* I tell you! We might have been rich. We might have rescued dear old Locust Hole from its sorry state."

She spun around to face August, who perched on a stool by the iron range. The boy thought the long-suffering handkerchief twisted in his aunt's fists might finally be torn in two.

"And you taped it to a model that you gave to . . . to Orchid? *Orchid?*" The lady's cheeks were flushed with horrified rage.

"I didn't know," pleaded August, with deep regret. "How

could I know? It was in a bag of marbles, and it looked just like . . . well . . . a *marble!*"

Hydrangea relented. She knew her nephew bore no blame.

"Orfeo must have camouflaged it," she said more calmly, shaking her head, "to conceal it from his creditors. He had that skull-shaped fossil sanded down into a sphere, polished up like glass, and then hid it in plain sight, right beneath our noses."

"I had it with me: the Zombie Stone," hissed August. "In the cemetery, when . . ." He nodded toward Claudette, who was nibbling at the planks blockading the window. "It must have drawn her spirit from the other place, back into the unfortunate, moldy body she left behind."

He placed his hands on his head.

"*That's* why she's here!"

His expression was one of mortified revelation.

"The Zombie Stone *made* her!"

"The Zombie Stone made her," repeated Hydrangea with wide eyes.

They faced each other in silent horror.

"At the party today"—August was suddenly filled with refreshed determination—"I have to fetch back that model. I need to send Claudette away. She's ruining my life. I *must* have the Zombie Stone!"

There was a fractured snapping from the other side of the room. Nephew and aunt watched as Claudette effortlessly wrenched a rusted nail from its board, dropped it onto her tongue, contemplated its flavor, then swallowed it.

"Things would be so much easier," whispered August confidentially, "if I were alone. But it's like she can sense where I am. It's impossible to shake her. And no door will hold her." He regarded the zombie with a sigh. "If, at least, she wasn't just so . . . *dead*-looking."

Hydrangea nodded sympathetically, gazing at the little zombie.

"I still have some of my gowns," she said thoughtfully, "from the old days." She drifted over to lift a lock of the girl's limp hair in her fingers. "A little hair spray, perhaps?" Claudette's eyes widened in alarm. "Now, don't you concern yourself, sugar," Hydrangea reassured her. "*I* am a Hurricane County Chili Pepper Princess title holder."

Taking the child's chin in her hand, the Chili Pepper Princess gently tilted Claudette's head this way and that. "And a little rouge? It's a challenge, to be sure." She glanced at August and shrugged. "But I think it might be done." She lit up with a wave of sudden enthusiasm. "A makeover, sugar; don't you think? It is, after all, *long* overdue!"

* * *

August and Claudette approached Château Malveau, funneled with many other arriving guests along the grand oak alley, toward the mansion's entrance.

The boy began to suspect that Hydrangea's makeover had failed to render Claudette less conspicuous, and worse, that it might have made her more so. For as they proceeded, heads were turning, and eyes were bulging. There were even a couple of stifled shrieks.

To be fair, the attention was not *only* directed toward Claudette. It's not every day, after all, one sees a diminutive beekeeper trailing twelve butterflies, accompanied by a lurching pageant princess in turquoise taffeta, with poufy bouffant hair and a grayish complexion emerging through makeup melting in the heat.

An aloof, long-nosed housemaid was greeting newcomers at the front door.

"Good day, madame, sir. Please come in."

But as she laid eyes on August and Claudette, her voice failed, her mouth opening and closing silently, like a goldfish.

"The festivities," she finally managed, "may be found on the rear lawn."

"My friend here," said August, leaning in confidentially, "has had a bit of a shock."

The housemaid leaned in too, painted-on eyebrows arched.

"An *electric* shock, sir?" she inquired without a shadow of a smile. "A faulty outlet, perhaps?"

"Um, yes. Something like that. Is there a quiet place where she might take a moment to recover?"

"You'll find the doors to the salon unlocked, sir. Just a short way down the hall, on the right. Everyone else is gathering out back."

She turned away, to welcome the following guest with equal disdain, and August slipped right past the salon where he had met the twins, instead pulling Claudette into the shadows of the staircase. The salty smell of boiling crawfish wafted through the passageway, accompanied by waves of raucous outdoor revelry: music, chatter, and laughter.

Behind them, the snooty housemaid was wrestling with an elderly lady's parasol and feather boa. Before them, the previous arrivals were passing onto the back veranda to wave at, greet, and join those guests thronging a broad, gracious lawn that swept down to the riverbank.

August roughly bundled Claudette across the wide, momentarily vacant hallway, to the chamber of jewels. He gripped a door lever.

"Please," he whispered, eyes closed, "don't be locked!"

It wasn't.

"Follow me," he hissed at Claudette. "The Zombie Stone is in here."

He quickly and quietly closed the door behind them. It took a moment for his eyes to adjust to the dim, eerie museum lighting. When they did, he confirmed that they were alone, then started immediately for the mantel.

But halfway across the room, August stopped in his tracks.

The potted fern had been returned to its original position. Of the skeleton boy and his balloon, there was no sign.

The Zombie Stone was gone.

August stood frozen. What to do next?

"Let's try the salon," he whispered, "then search the other . . ."

He spun back to Claudette to find a familiar, neckless silhouette in the doorway.

"Mister August?" said the butler's snooty voice. "Did you lose yourself?"

It was perfectly obvious that August had not.

"Bernice informs me," continued Escargot, "that the young lady arrived feeling out of sorts. Has she . . . been revived?"

August, embarrassed by the discovered trespass, nodded meekly.

"Then I must inform you that Mister Beauregard impatiently awaits you to commence an activity he describes as . . . *paintball*."

Escargot indicated the proposed route with a gloved hand.

"The party, sir, is *this* way."

CHAPTER 29

THE BELONGING

It was two hours later, and the entire world had changed.

Or at least August DuPont's had.

The boy sat at one of the long trestle tables set up on the riverbank, surrounded by Beauregard's friends and a gaggle of other boisterous, laughing young people. Traces of dried yellow paint crusted the netting of his protective helmet. His sleeve was torn, and a nasty bruise was darkening his elbow. He remained daunted by the rowdy, pressing mass of bodies, and his throat was raw from yelling over the din.

But in his entire life, August had never been so happy.

He would have ventured to guess that even the season winner of *Word or Number?* (who had walked away with a three-day hot-air balloon tour of active volcanoes) could not have felt such perfect contentment. Indeed, the universe itself seemed to sense August's soaring joy, for everything around him was celebration.

On a makeshift stage beneath a flapping marquee, a live band was making wild, infectious, foot-tapping music, with fiddles and a squeezebox and a strange, corrugated metal vest that the wearer strummed with laughing abandon.

And as the evening air finally cooled, and the sky turned orange behind the mansion, the assembly had responded to the festive rhythms by taking to the dance floor. Cowboy hats were bobbing, skirts were swirling, and boots were stomping, all with energetic zeal.

But no dancer was more enthused than Claudette the zombie.

Jerking her stiff little limbs, she reeled recklessly about, an ecstatic grin from ear to ear, narrowly avoiding collision at every turn.

The "activity described as paintball," as it transpired, had saved the day.

Splashed and splotched with multicolored pigment from head to foot, Claudette had been inadvertently camouflaged, indistinguishable from the other spattered paintball participants. And while many had since cleaned themselves up a bit, the zombie's appearance was still far less remarkable than it had been upon her arrival.

August stifled a mischievous smile. It was hard to imagine . . . but they were getting away with it.

He was jolted by a hearty slap on the back.

"How's your elbow, Cousin?" inquired Beauregard. Unlike his sweaty guests, Beauregard had changed into fresh clothes. Other than a faint pink stain in his hair, he was restored to his pristine, gentlemanly self.

August assured him that his elbow and general well-being were never better.

"Jeez!" Beauregard exclaimed. "That Laplander sure has some constitution."

They watched Claudette careening through the other dancers' legs.

"She didn't even seem to *feel* those pellets. Just kept charging through them, like they were snowflakes. I saw one go right in her mouth. She didn't even spit it out!"

Beauregard waved Claudette toward them, and as she staggered over, he patted the space on the bench beside him.

"You fancy yourself some crawfish, Miz Claudette? How about some gumbo?"

"Oh!" blurted August hastily, anxious to avoid any further display of Claudette's unusual table manners. "She only eats whale blubber. And frozen turnips."

"And spoons occasionally," said Beauregard with an arched brow but a good-natured smile.

Claudette giggled and shrugged.

"Give it here," said August. "I'll have her gumbo."

As the spicy stew warmed his throat, August happily absorbed the party around him. And then there was a moment—a single, incredible moment—when something magical happened.

Behind August, dancers scooted and jigged in a blur of motion. Before him, Gaston and Langley were thumb-wrestling. Belladonna peered into her phone, scowling. Claudette tossed empty peanut shells into her own mouth.

The closing scene, his favorite scene, the scene that meant everything from the *Stella Starz* credits, was unfolding in real life—and August was *in* it. A warm feeling formed in the boy's toes, ran up his legs, and coursed through his entire being.

It was elation. This was it. Like Stella, August was at last— at long, long last—starring in his own life. *Finally,* he'd arrived at that yearned-for place, a place with friends, friends who accepted him as one of their own.

At last, August *belonged.*

In what shenanigans would *his* gang participate? Would they deliver the school bully her just rewards? Reveal that the cafeteria ghost was in fact a disgruntled cook? Or perhaps they'd craftily orchestrate the unlikely but perfect romantic pairing of soccer coach to drama teacher.

He felt that twitch in his right hand.

It was time.

Buoyant with happiness, August faced Beauregard, swung his hand into the air, and opened his palm.

But Beauregard didn't see him.

Beauregard was leaning over his plate, attracting the attention of his fellow diners.

"Guys. *Guys!* Listen up!"

With some shushing and nudging, the immediate company fell silent.

"So," announced Beauregard with a conspiratorial grin as Gaston, Langley, Claudette, and several other young people leaned in to better hear the charismatic boy speak. "I have some news. Juicy gossip."

August experienced an inexplicable shiver of apprehension. Something was wrong. He glanced up at the mansion, recalling his mission to locate the Zombie Stone.

"Claudette here"—Beauregard eyed the girl beside him— "has herself a little secret."

August's heart skipped a beat.

"She's not a Laplander at all. Isn't that so, Miz Claudette?"

Beauregard gripped Claudette's shoulder and gave it an affable shake. Between the paintball and the dancing, the undead girl's parts had become a little, let's say . . . loosened. Beauregard's jovial jostling was the last straw.

With a wet *plop!*, Claudette's loose eyeball shot from its socket, fell to the table, rolled across the checkered cloth, and came to rest against a bottle of Malveau's Devil Sauce.

196

Startled by the disturbance, a two-inch centipede scuttled out of her right nostril.

There was stunned silence.

But it was momentary.

Suddenly Langley emitted a shrill, hysterical, ear-piercing sound.

"It's a zombie!" he screamed.

CHAPTER 30

THE BETRAYAL

August experienced the next several seconds almost as if he were watching a slow-motion playback. And in times to come, when he remembered the events, it would always play out in his mind the same way.

Limbs flailed lazily, and hair drifted through the air, like it might in water. The bench beneath him slowly tilted and fell, as diners lunged gracefully away from the table. The sounds of panic blended into one long, groaning yawn.

But then his mind and the moment resynced, and everything around him was fast and loud and terrible. He picked himself off the ground and saw his helmet nearby, crushed in the stampede.

He was surrounded by gaping faces. Those who had sought to gain distance had collided with those who had drawn closer to observe, and all were now collected in a circle, some fifteen feet in radius. At its center were August and Claudette.

The dancing and music had ceased. Beyond the crowd, August spotted the band members standing on tiptoe, attempting to catch a glimpse of the drama.

And there was a voice, speaking loudly. It was a voice he knew, and yet it sounded altered and strange. It was Beauregard's voice.

"I knew it the moment I shook its hand," he was crowing, turning full circle to address the entire audience, "and felt that cold and lifeless grip. It's not an exchange student." He pointed at Claudette with a righteous index finger. "It's a filthy dirty zombie!"

Who was this person? He *looked* like Beauregard. He shared his perfect oval face and broad, embracing smile. His eyes were wide-set, of dark, translucent brown like tea. And yet there was something unfamiliar in them. They twinkled not with mischievous humor, but with . . . yes, with *malice*.

Had they changed? Or had August simply misread them all along?

Beauregard snatched up Claudette's eyeball from the table and grimaced at its slippery texture. He darted over to the wall of spectators and waved the dripping sphere in their faces, eliciting shrieks of horror that made his grin broaden, a grin that, once devilish, suddenly seemed demonic.

Claudette lunged at the boy, intent on retrieving her organ. But Beauregard, far taller than she, simply held it out of reach, laughing as the small zombie awkwardly lurched and jumped, grunting in frustration.

"Langley!" cried Beauregard. "Heads up!" The eyeball sailed through the air.

"Ew!" squealed Langley, tossing it on to Gaston.

"Gaston, to me!" Beauregard raised his open hand.

And thus, a cruel game of catch ensued.

Langley and Gaston were not entirely heartless young men, but sadly, they were the sort who were too lazy to think for themselves. It was far easier and more comfortable to leave the decisions to Beauregard, and to do his bidding, for which they received his praise and friendship, which gave them a sense of security.

To give him some credit, Gaston frowned as if experiencing a pang of guilt at the sight of the lumbering zombie. But on catching a glimpse of Beauregard's thunderous expression . . . he tossed the eyeball.

August watched the scene, an entirely new emotion mounting within him. He realized what it must be; he'd seen Stella

Starz exhibit it only once, when her father had dropped to one knee and proposed to the surly, scheming Hedwig.

It was anger.

Claudette was increasingly distressed, tripping over her own feet and wailing mournfully as the eyeball repeatedly arced across her head.

August's anger combusted into fury.

He put an end to the whole thing quickly and simply, by stepping forward and reaching up to intercept the small globe in midflight. There was silence as Beauregard contemplated him with narrow eyes . . . then lifted his open palm.

"Throw it!" he said quietly with a slight sneer.

August knew in an instant that the words represented both an offer and a threat: participate in the callous teasing, and remain in Beauregard's good graces. Or . . .

August looked at Claudette. Her eye socket looked particularly vacant, framed as it was by the green and orange paint streaking her face. Spittle was foaming at the corners of her panting mouth. She was a disaster.

Next he looked at Beauregard: all symmetry, cleanliness, and dashing smile. He thought of the future lunchtime gatherings. He thought of the back slapping and arm punching. He thought of the potential adventures: the undoing of bullies, the exposing of spies, the recovery of penguins.

He thought of the belonging.

August pulled his arm back to throw.

But on glancing again at Claudette, he froze. The girl's face had collapsed into an expression of grief and betrayal. It looked for all the world as if her cold, un-beating heart was breaking.

"Over here, August!" called Beauregard encouragingly.

August thought of Claudette's adoring gaze during her first embrace, the same look she had bestowed upon her brother in that long-ago photograph. He thought about her eagerness to model for someone's grotesque tattoo. He thought about her patient, agreeable assistance in hunting down the Zombie Stone.

The boy lowered his arm and extended his hand toward the zombie, and the eyeball was restored to its rightful owner, whose face transformed, like a Christmas tree lit up for the first time.

Beauregard approached like a slinking coyote, with a small, awful smile. August feared the worst was yet to come.

"You knew it all along," Beauregard said in a low, dangerous voice, "didn't you, August? Laplander, my rear end! You enjoy the company of the undead, August? You like the smell of rot and decay?"

His nose was inches from that of the boy who had defied him.

"You a zombie lover, August?"

Beauregard placed the tips of his fingers against August's shoulder and shoved, hard, so that August stumbled backward.

There was a spine-chilling sound, half howl, half roar.

Like a cannonball, the small zombie shot forward and grabbed Beauregard by the front of his crisply ironed vest. He hadn't even a chance to scream before he was lifted clear off the ground and hurled, like a limp strand of spaghetti, through the air to crash into the picnic table, which collapsed beneath him.

Beauregard sat momentarily stunned in the wreckage of crawfish, gumbo, and half-eaten corncobs. But the amazed expression was quickly replaced by something ominous, dark, and hateful.

"Did you see that?" he cried with outrage, appealing to the surrounding throng. "It's violent! Zombies are dangerous, unhygienic creatures that have no place in decent society." He awkwardly scrambled to his feet, unaware that a crawfish claw protruded from the breast pocket of his expensive jacket.

"It didn't occur to me for a second," he seethed at August, "that you were ever—how did you put it?—perfectly *normal.*"

Beauregard drew himself to full height, reclaiming his dignity and asserting his superiority.

"I knew from the moment I laid eyes on your owlish head and ridiculous butterflies that you were anything but normal. Like your demented aunt. Like *all* the DuPonts, crazier than a forkful of soup: one generation of freaks after the next working toward a well-deserved ruination."

He chuckled bitterly.

"I still can't believe you bought it. You *actually* thought that I wanted to be friends, when all I really wanted from you . . . was this." He gestured at the surrounding spectators. "A little summer fun with the ghost of Locust Hole.

"You *actually* imagined that the likes of you might belong at Château Malveau. A zombie-loving DuPont belong with *us?*"

He dropped his voice to a level that only August could hear and hissed like a serpent, "You will never belong. *Never!*"

CHAPTER 31

A CATASTROPHIC MISUNDERSTANDING

August felt light-headed, and his legs scarcely held him up. The open smiles. The shoulder shaking. The arm thumping. The jokes and invitations and promises of camaraderie. It had all been a lie. From the very beginning it had all been one long setup.

August had been nothing more than Beauregard's plaything, an ill-fated mouse to an indifferent house cat, ultimately lured to his own doom.

Beauregard was not his friend.

There were no friends.

There was no belonging.

The surrounding faces confirmed everything, filled as they were with repulsion and derision. They were faces that clearly regarded August as an outsider, an unsavory oddity.

If you are saddened by the lack of compassion in such a large gathering of people, please take heart. There were, in fact, many expressions of pity and concern in the crowd, but August simply did not see them.

Sometimes emotions run so high, they affect our vision. August viewed the scene through the filter of his own despair, and it appeared correspondingly bleak. One reaction in particular burned itself into the boy's memory and came to represent everything August saw around him in that moment. It was the reaction of Belladonna Malveau.

Her brow furrowed deeply, her jaw jutted forward. Disgust and something close to loathing twisted her pearly mouth into an ugly sneer. He couldn't hear her, but he saw the word her lips formed.

"Disgusting!"

And thus, the boy arrived at another new emotion. As anger had been fiery and forceful, so this one was thick and cold and burdensome.

It was shame.

He was, apparently, disgusting.

August could not bear the sensation for another moment.

With one hand, he shielded his face and burning unshed tears. With the other, he grabbed Claudette's arm and, pursued by a gaggle of butterflies, dragged her into the crowd.

A path appeared before them, as partygoers hurriedly scrambled out of their way. The pair might have even made a full escape in merely seconds, had they not been confronted by an obstacle blocking the route.

August stopped short before colliding with it and looked up to see a slender figure with honey-blond hair draped from head to toe in a glittering black veil.

* * *

August obediently took a seat in one of the high-backed chairs, while Claudette wandered aimlessly around the Chamber of Jewels, examining—and occasionally licking—the specimen jars.

Orchid observed the girl with a strange expression—partly of distaste, but also fascination. She laid down her palmetto fan and leaned forward in the other chair.

"So, child," she said in that creamy voice, transfixed by Claudette, "you located the Zombie Stone." It was a statement rather than a question.

August was shaken from his misery by surprise.

"You know," he said with a puzzled frown, "that Orfeo's Cadaverite was known as the Zombie Stone?"

"Everyone knows *that*." Orchid delivered a now familiar response.

"Everyone it seems, but me."

"It's how Orfeo created his infamous zombie act. And I must therefore conclude, from the presence of this . . . undead creature, that you have found the means of her making: the Zombie Stone. Yes?"

She turned eagerly to August, the rose lips curving like a crescent moon.

"Have you brought it with you, dear boy?"

"Um . . . well, you see, you already have it in your possession, ma'am."

Orchid gave a puzzled chuckle.

"Now, what on earth could you mean?"

"The model I gave you," explained August. "The balloon formed by a marble? It is made of Alligator Eye. Cadaverite. It is the Zombie Stone."

There was a pause, and a frown creased the lovely forehead. Then suddenly she was out of her chair and gripping August's upper arms with urgency and surprising strength.

"That *skeleton* model?" He could feel her breath and smell the heady fragrance of gardenias. "*That* contained the Zombie Stone?"

August nodded, a little frightened by the wildness in the woman's eyes.

"Where is it?" August said in a very small voice, unsure if he wanted the answer.

Orchid straightened, shaking her head in disbelief.

"Do you have any idea of that stone's worth? Do you comprehend what I have lost?"

"Lost?" repeated August, wincing in anticipation.

"Belladonna sold some of her ridiculous pasta jewelry to an equally ridiculous art dealer from Croissant City. He saw your . . . *sculpture* . . . here, and took an inexplicable liking to it."

Orchid looked unsteady and grabbed at the mantel for support.

"This is a catastrophe!" she said, looking around the room as if it might yield some unexpected solution. "I sold the thing for a pittance."

She looked directly at August with a face of unbridled horror.

"I *sold* the Zombie Stone!"

CHAPTER 32

THE EVIL TWIN

It was a strange and gloomy sort of birthday celebration.

August, Hydrangea, and Claudette were gathered around Locust Hole's closet-door dining table, each sporting a paper party hat. A squirming column of smoke rose from a recently extinguished candle, which protruded from a cake of creamy swirls.

Hydrangea served each diner a slice. They ate in silence until the lady laid down her fork and opened her mouth.

"I know!" snapped August before she could speak. "Beauregard betrayed me, as Orchid betrayed you, as every Malveau has betrayed every DuPont since Maxim stole Pierre's recipe. The world is cruel and full of butterflies and betrayals, and you told me so all along."

Hydrangea raised her eyes and they were shining. She looked very sad, and August instantly regretted his outburst.

"I was merely going to wish you," said Hydrangea quietly, "a happy birthday, sugar."

August apologized, and Hydrangea assured him there was no need, that indeed she understood his feelings all too well. And August knew that she did.

"I hope you like the cream cheese cake, sugar. I sold another crate of hot sauce, so we might celebrate in style. There are only a few boxes remaining, and then . . ." Her voice trailed off, and she pushed the food around her plate despondently.

Claudette left her seat, went to Hydrangea, and gently patted her unkempt hair. Hydrangea smiled up at her gratefully.

"Don't worry, Aunt," said August. "We'll figure something out."

"Will we?"

But August was saved from lying by the sound of the doorbell.

* * *

Now that he was a more-frequent visitor to the outside world, August had persuaded Hydrangea to unbarricade the front door. The boy had installed an unemployed screen door from the kitchen to prevent the invasion of winged insects.

And so, August was able to greet the visitor at full height—that visitor being, he discovered, Belladonna Malveau.

She was, as usual, quite terrifying, glaring at him through the screen with quiet ferocity. Fearing another ruthless tongue-lashing, August quickly closed the door. But just before it met the frame, August heard the words "I'm sorry!" And they were said with sincerity.

August was so surprised that he instinctively opened the door a little and cautiously observed the visitor through the gap.

"About my brother, I mean," explained Belladonna. "Beau-regard has grown into a vicious snob. I would have warned you. I *should* have warned you." She looked contrite. "But he's so charming, no one ever believes me. At least, not at first." She sighed sadly. "And to be honest, I didn't think he would sink so low. His behavior yesterday was *disgusting*!" She half spat the word.

Disgusting.

August's head spun. Nothing was as he had thought. He realized that he knew even less than he imagined.

It was at Beauregard that Belladonna's scorn had been directed, both at the crawfish boil and before that. The eye rolls, the sneers, and the frosty demeanor had never been meant for August. It was her own twin that Belladonna found disgusting.

August opened the door fully.

"When there are twins," he said thoughtfully, "one of them

is always evil." And at Belladonna's puzzled look: "Just something someone told me once."

"Is that your zombie?" Belladonna was peering into the gloom over August's shoulder. Claudette was lurking protectively in the foyer behind him, growling like a cornered alley cat. Belladonna gave the zombie an unexpected, if reserved, little wave. The snarling ceased.

"You've been experimenting with color," observed August as Belladonna's bracelet passed close to his face. The jewelry was predictably black, except for a single piece of orecchiette, which was lacquered in a brilliant, glossy scarlet.

Belladonna hesitated. "You're aware that ours is a house of eternal mourning." She gazed off to one side, contemplating something or other. "One can grow weary of grieving for things lost. Of broken hearts. Of shuttered windows and covered mirrors." She turned and looked August in the eye. "Of black."

She fingered the solitary piece of scarlet pasta.

"I'm reminded," said August, looking from the bracelet to its maker, "that you deserve congratulations . . . on your recent sale."

Belladonna brightened a little.

"The art dealer," she explained, "was taking a tour of the mansion, and apparently my jewelry caught his eye. He described it as irresistibly depressing."

"How wonderful!" August's brow creased in thought. "Do

you happen to recall the name of the dealer's gallery in Croissant City?"

"How funny. Mama asked me that very same question. But I couldn't remember." Belladonna pursed her lips, clearly racking her brain. "Something to do with macaroni perhaps. Or macramé?" She shook her head. "Sorry; I'm not sure."

They fell into an awkward silence. August could not think of anything more to say. Belladonna suddenly produced a letter—which, apparently, she'd had in her possession the entire time—and handed it to August.

"The Malveaus are a queer bunch," she said, regarding the boy sadly. "You're likely better off without us. Good luck to you, August."

And with that, she turned and gingerly made her way down the splintered porch steps. And August opened the envelope to see a familiar gold family crest depicting a chili pepper impaled on a fancy-handled dagger.

Dear August,

The Zombie Stone remains in the possession of someone other than myself. Despite I'm sure the best of intentions, you have failed to uphold your end of our agreement.

I feel certain, then, that you cannot expect me to uphold mine. In short, you will not be

*attending school in New Madrid with Beauregard
and Belladonna next month.*

*You may take comfort in learning that after
yesterday's grotesque and vulgar incident, I
intend, in any case, to save the twins from further
embarrassment by enrolling them at an academy
far from here, in Croissant City.*

*Home tutelage at the hands of your aunt
Hydrangea, and a generally low profile, perhaps
represents the best option for you after all.*

Sincerely,

Orchid Malveau

CHAPTER 33

ALONE ... AGAIN

August and Claudette perched at the edge of the gazebo, their feet resting on the mossy submerged steps. A handful of the braver minnows had ventured beyond the sunken canoe and were considering the zombie's toes as a source of dinner.

August's trampled helmet had been left at Château Malveau, so he was bareheaded, but neither child seemed to even notice the resulting assembly of butterflies. On the canal, where Madame Marvell's crooked houseboat had rocked just hours before, there now buzzed only a pair of courting dragonflies.

August fished a limp, dripping sheet of paper from the canal and passed it to Claudette. She cocked her head in an effort to comprehend the notice. August helpfully reached over and turned the paper right way up. The zombie threw him a quizzical look and burbled wetly. August thought he detected a question in the throaty, foamy sound.

"It's from the Department of Child Services," he explained. "It's addressed to Madame Delfine Marvell. I guess that's *our* Madame Marvell's grandmother. It says they're dropping by tomorrow to discuss the minor they believe to be living on board."

Claudette's eyes bulged, and August nodded.

"I don't know how they found her all the way out here, but I guess she moved on. I reckon they'll never catch up to her."

August shooed a butterfly from his nose and gazed down the canal, through a cloud of glittering no-see-ums. For a moment, far off where the canal opened into Black River, he perhaps saw something break the water's surface—something very long and very pale. Was it the giant reptile of recent report? Or was the rumor nothing more than a titillating fancy, like the ghost of Locust Hole? Likely he—and perhaps everyone else—had seen nothing more than ripples sparkling in the late-summer sunlight.

"I could have run away with her," mused August. "Or sailed away, I suppose. To Croissant City, to find that gallery named Macaroni. Or Macramé." He shook his head. "But how could I do that now, alone?"

The boy settled his face on his knees, and the weight of his solitude bore down upon him. He'd been returned to the friendless state he'd suffered before the party, before the arrogant Malveaus, before the mysterious houseboat had materialized.

Even Stella Starz, he realized with a wave of misery, had left him, spirited away in Madame Marvell's mustard plastic television. No more ill-advised escapades. No more intimate lunches. No more high fives.

The thought was nearly unbearable.

"Alone," he sighed raggedly, in deep despair. "Again."

He was jolted rudely from his self-pity by a shove from Claudette. August looked up wearily and was surprised to find the zombie frowning. She jabbed her thumb crossly into her own chest.

"Oh," said August, abashed, "of course! Yes. There's you, Claudette. My apologies; I suppose the undead are people too, right?"

Smiling sadly, August rose to leave. But Claudette grasped his forearm. He recalled the first time she'd grabbed him and how frightened he had been. Now, that long-ago reaction seemed so unjustified, so silly.

Claudette raised her finger, as if to say "Hold on a moment."

"Yes?" said August, eyebrows raised.

Claudette stood and, oblivious to her freshly washed and mended burial dress, descended the steps into the shallows, scattering minnows in all directions. She reached into the water and, tossing a slime-covered rope over her shoulder, began with little effort to pull. Behind her, onto the grassy bank beside the gazebo, slithered the sunken canoe, water spouting from holes in its sides.

The girl pointed at the canoe. She pointed at August. She pointed at herself. She pointed down the canal, toward the river.

"You want us to row a patched-up canoe," laughed August, half-amused, half-incredulous, "all the way to Croissant City?"

The zombie flexed her biceps.

"You're serious, aren't you?" August shook his head in wonder. "You are, I must confess, crazy strong."

Claudette grinned.

August grinned too. Were they really going to do this?

Suddenly the small zombie swung her open palm into the air.

August hesitated for a second, then smacked it heartily with his own.

And just like that, for the first time in his life, August DuPont exchanged a high five.

EPILOGUE

One hundred and seven miles east of Locust Hole's gazebo, at the heart of boisterous, colorful Croissant City, lay a curious little store. It occupied a leafy, shaded alley so narrow, it was rarely noticed or explored by the throngs of passing tourists.

Those that did venture off the sunny avenue discovered, halfway down, a tiny house dwarfed by neighboring structures of grander design. The storefront had a single door and a single window, and the shutters of these covered most of the visible, crumbling stucco. A small hinged sign hung from the eaves that read "Leech's Camera Botanica."

Inside, the intrepid explorer would discover a space more cramped even than the exterior might suggest. The low ceiling

lay somewhere behind clouds of drying herbs and plants. The walls were entirely concealed by a boggling array of labeled jars and bottles filled with a rainbow of powders and potions. In the deepest recesses of the store, behind the stand of books about spells and magic, hung a black velvet curtain.

At the very moment that August's and Claudette's palms high-fived back at Locust Hole, an unearthly blue light was escaping from around the edges of that curtain, and voices were drifting from the chamber it concealed.

"You claim to have experience in necromancy, Mr. Leech?" said the sturdy lady with coiffed pink-gray hair and a large purse.

"*Professor* Leech," the man opposite corrected her politely with a pointed look over his thick black spectacles. "I believe you will find no one in this state more skilled in the dark arts, madame."

They were the only people in the space. Indeed, it could not have accommodated more, for it was mostly filled by a draped table and the two occupied chairs. A shelf on the rear wall was crowded with bric-a-brac, reminiscent of a certain cluttered table on a certain perilous houseboat: jelly jars filled with keys or candies, a silver bowl of silver coins, yellow candles.

All was bathed in the milky luminance emanating from the

mists swirling at the center of a large crystal ball resting on the table.

"What do you see, Mr. . . . I mean Professor?"

Professor Leech was peering into the luminous sphere. Lit from beneath, the shadows of his round, babyish face took on a horror movie appearance.

"Do you see my husband? Do you see my Henri?"

Silence.

"Do you see anything at all, Professor?"

"Oh, rest assured, madame, I see something." The professor's bulbous, pug-like eyes remained intensely focused on some scene visible only to him. "In all my years in this field, I have, in fact, never received a vision so vivid, so clear."

"Is it Henri come to me from the other world? What does he say?"

The professor sat back, removed his glasses, and wiped them.

"It is not your husband, madame," he said apologetically. "In fact, I can hardly believe this message is for you. Which means"—his brow furrowed in puzzlement—"it must be . . . for *me.*"

"For *you?*" snapped the woman, surprised and a little irritated. "Well, that's a fine thing! What makes you think so? What do you see?"

The professor fixed the woman's gaze, and she saw something unexpected in his eyes. Was it excitement?

"I see an alligator," said the professor, "of extraordinary length; perhaps forty feet, or more. It is pure white . . . and it is headed this way!"